THE WILDER SIDE OF CHAOS

An action-packed crime thriller with a stunning ending

PETE BRASSETT

THE
BOOK
FOLKS

Paperback published by The Book Folks

London, 2019

© Pete Brassett

This book is a work of fiction. Names, characters,
businesses, organizations, places and events are either the
product of the author's imagination or are used fictitiously.
Any resemblance to actual persons, living or dead, events
or locales is entirely coincidental. The spelling is British
English.

ISBN 978-1-6956-7556-8

www.thebookfolks.com

For the Cash man.
Mad as a box of frogs
with eyes in the back of his head.
Which is where he needed them most.

Chapter One

'Death's a path that must be trod,
if man would ever pass to God.'

Thomas Parnell

The night, like Indian ink, was tinged with purple. A cloudless sky was peppered with tiny pinholes of light. Fireflies danced in the distance and the sound of distant drums carried across the plains. He experienced, momentarily, a humbling feeling of immense insignificance. He felt the shackles of Samsara fall away.

The crackle of the fire shook him from his reverie. He smiled to himself and started back the fifty yards or so to camp. With nightfall came a sharp drop in temperature and there was already a noticeable nip in the air.

For the second time in as many days, he burned his hands as he pulled the pot from the fire. His attempt to cool them by blowing was nothing more than a futile, psychological gesture. The dull throbbing in his palms was soon forgotten as the aroma of chilli took charge of his remaining senses. It smelled good, no doubt enriched by the weevils that had dropped to the pot from the tree above where they had sought sanctuary from the heat of the day.

He uncorked the wine, filled a chipped, white enamel mug and passed it to her. Flames danced in her emerald eyes; her skin, once as white as porcelain, glistened brown – tanned by the searing heat of the midday sun. The hair that used to frame her chiselled features was scraped back in a practical ponytail. She smiled softly as she took the mug.

The fire hissed as he spat the chilli out. Her laughter broke the silence.

'Eejit!' she whispered in her soft Kerry brogue. 'You should've let it cool down.'

He nodded in affirmation. They ate, huddled together, enveloped by the night; surrounded by the sound of chirping crickets and the last dying gasps of the fire. Their thoughts turned to sleep. They would leave at sunrise.

Inside the tent, safe from the attention of ravenous mosquitoes, they shed their clothes and let the cool, night air caress their bodies. The softness of her lips brought forth a genuine sigh of well-being from somewhere deep within his soul. They lay still, motionless, her head on his chest, her being safe in his encircling arms. She was the happiest she'd ever been, blissfully unaware that never again would she see a smile crack his weathered face. Never again would she hear his voice call her name. Never again would she tremble at his very touch.

* * *

It was barely light when she was awoken, not as she had thought, by the cold of the night, but by the marble-like iciness of his chest. Her piercing scream, like the blood-curdling cry of a hyrax, forced the bustards to flight, leaving the acacias bowing, as if agitated by a storm wind.

Gripped at once by fear and the bowel-stirring reality of what confronted her, she fought desperately to free herself from his vice-like grip. Frantically, she backed away and curled up in a protective ball, staring in disbelief at the corpse that lay before her.

She swallowed hard as waves of nausea washed over her body. Trembling hands toyed erratically with her hair. She shivered spasmodically and screamed again as tears flowed down her terror-stricken cheeks. Her mind raced with irrational thoughts and selfish questions: How could he do this to her? How he could leave her? Why did he pull her insides out and torment her with visions of loneliness?

She reached out, nervously, and traced the line of his nose with her index finger. Softly, she stroked his forehead and gently brushed his hair back. Eventually the tears waned and she lay down beside him. She held him, tightly, and closed her eyes.

* * *

The muffled voices beyond the tent shattered her solitude. Two, maybe three. Men. They were speaking Swahili. She was scared, frightened and painfully aware that in death he had robbed her of the confidence she had taken to bed just a few hours earlier. She wiped the salt from her cheeks, pulled on one of his tee-shirts and cautiously ventured outside. Three ebony silhouettes stood tall before her. Their lean figures belied their strength, their broad shoulders the only indication of some athletic prowess. They grinned simultaneously, flashing teeth like polished ivory, while their yellow eyes scanned her petite frame with interest. They bowed their heads and squatted on the ground; it was obvious they meant no harm. They were Masai. The eldest of the three coyly examined his fingernails as he spoke.

'Jambo, Miss Jambo. I don't wish to intrude but we heard your cries. Do you need help? Tell me what is wrong. Please, let us help you.'

His Oxford intonation was ridiculously incongruous.

'What? You're, you're English! Holy Mother of God! I mean, you...'

'Actually, I am Kenyan and proud of it, but yes, I do speak the Queen's English. I suppose I am what you might call an educated man! My name is Joseph, Joseph Ndambiki, and these are my brothers. Do you have any tea?'

* * *

The very concept of taking tea with an Oxford-educated Masai warrior was at best bizarre, but nonetheless, re-assuring. Comforting. She couldn't help but trust these men, she had to, she needed them.

She rambled, sometimes incoherently, in an effort to explain, to rationalise, to justify, the situation. She knew not how, nor why, nor when Nat had passed away, only that he was gone. Joseph listened intently and reassured her with an occasional nod of the head. He appeared to comprehend the situation perfectly.

'Well, Miss,' he began, 'a doctor of medicine I am not, but one thing is certain: the body of your beloved will not keep long in this heat. We must get him to Mombasa, to the consulate, at once.'

'Mombasa?' she said.

'Of course, Nairobi is too far. I can assure you the authorities there will treat him better than the sun! Come, I will ride with you, it will be quicker.'

'What? Now? Oh, I... thanks. Thank you. I don't, I don't know what to say. I've not even told you my name.'

She held out her hand; it seemed like the right thing to do.

'It's... I'm Jack. Jacky. People call me Jack.'

'Well, we must hurry, Miss Jack, we don't have long.'

* * *

Joseph and his brothers lifted the body and placed it gently in the back of the Land Cruiser. Neither they, nor Jack, noticed the tiny wound behind his left ear – a tiny puncture mark. The kind of mark only a needle could make.

Jack placed her hand on his brow and took a long, last look at his face. She smiled as Joseph covered him with a sheet. Her eyes glazed over.

'Do you know how we met?' she asked.

Chapter Two

'He either fears his fate too much,
or his deserts are small,
That dares not put it to the touch,
to gain or lose it all.'

Marquis of Montrose

The rain hammered against the window. The cold, grey wash of the morning sky cast a chilling aura throughout the apartment and filled each tiny room with an eerie sense of gloom.

He woke, as usual, before the alarm could sound, scratched his groin and took comfort in the sound of the deluge outside. It had no rhythm, there was no pit-a-pat. It was erratic, like jazz. It was jazz rain. Rain suited him, he liked it; he preferred it in fact to the heat of the city during the summer, when tempers flared and the drains smelled. It was ten after six when eventually he rose and padded his way to the bathroom.

'Nathan,' he told his crumpled reflection, 'you should take a break.'

He rubbed his chin and sneered at his likeness. The stubble, he convinced himself, could wait. He showered leisurely and returned to the lounge where he sat in the window and sipped Tropicana from the carton.

He sparked his first Marlboro of the day and watched as the denizens of the Rue de Jarente, three floors below, went about their business. Monsieur L'Argent, the middle-aged widower who resembled Jacques Tatie, headed for another day at the bank, Homburg pulled down over his face, collar turned up against the elements. Mademoiselle Baiser, blessed with curves like an hour-glass, waved adieu to another guest from the shelter of her doorway. Nat contemplated her chosen profession. It wasn't in his nature to cast aspersions, but he couldn't help but wonder if it had anything to do with her obviously insatiable libido. Henri la Vache, the butcher from the Rue St. Antoine, sped by in his Citroën and tooted his horn at the sight of the young mademoiselle. It was Nat's cue to dress and leave for the office.

Despite his love of the rain, he was never prepared for it. He never wore a cap, nor did he own an umbrella. 'You get wet, you get dry' was his attitude to inclement weather. He enjoyed wet.

Ten minutes later, damp but not soaked, he arrived at the counter of his local bar. How people could survive without coffee was beyond him. He raised his cup in a mock toast to the drenched traffic cops who sat huddled in the corner.

'Plaîsir de la moto, eh!' he said.

The comment was returned with an expletive and a smile. It was the kind of exchange only good-humoured acquaintances could enjoy. The sanitation workers at the next table roared with laughter as they raised their Calvados and returned the toast with a hearty 'Salut!'

* * *

He stubbed out his cigarette with a swift twist of the foot and signalled his goodbye with a simple wave of the hand. As he crossed the Pont St. Louis, he observed that, even in the rain, there was a beauty that only the Seine could offer. Unlike the Thames, it was accessible, approachable. It was a part of the city and not an obstacle that cut a swathe through its heart.

He sauntered along the Rue de Vaugirard and stopped just past Le Jardin de Luxembourg to afford himself a glance up at his studio, at the sign that read 'Citron'. He wrinkled his brow and sniffed. It was three years since he founded the company and it was the longest he'd ever remained in any one job, but 'Citron' was beginning to taste bitter. He wasn't a businessman; he didn't enjoy running a company. He needed change.

He shrugged his shoulders, sighed and crossed the street. He was uncharacteristically startled by the sight of a sodden, gamine figure cowering in the doorway. He studied her intently. Drops of rainwater hung heavy on the longest lashes he'd ever seen and her green eyes sparkled despite the lack of sunshine. She'd been there long enough for a pool of water to gather at her feet.

* * *

'Ça-va?' he asked tersely as he opened the door, half expecting a plea for money.

'Sorry, I don't speak... parlez-vous Anglais? English? Monsieur Pearson? Je m'appelle Jack, Jacky Caragh... oh shite...'

Nat regarded her with a look of contempt, as though her efforts were totally wasted on him. It was the first time he'd heard French spoken with an Irish accent. She looked vulnerable, scared; as if she wanted to run away.

'Okay, you'd better come in and dry off, eh?'

'What? You're not Fre..! You made me go through all that when...'

'Yeah. Tough, eh? C'mon, we'll get you some coffee, find you somewhere warm to wait.'

His roguish grin was returned in kind, their gaze lasting just long enough to avoid embarrassment. He showed her to an office where she sat and waited, perched on the edge of a leather couch. He gave it ten minutes before returning. She stood as the door opened. Her damp fringe fell across her elfin features.

'Better?' asked Nat as he strode across the room.

'Much, thanks.' she said nervously. 'What time will he come? Mr Pearson, I mean. Probably quite late I imagine, I mean, being the boss and all.'

'Nat, late? You're kidding. He's up with the birds, hardly sleeps if you ask me. Word of advice though, call him Nathan, or Nat, he prefers that. He ain't one for formalities, not Nat.'

He tossed his jacket on the floor, sat at the desk and lit another cigarette. She shuffled nervously and hesitated before speaking.

'Well, no offence like, but I think I'll wait to hear that from him. What'll he think if he walks in here and has me calling him by his first name and all. I'd like this to be more than just a day trip, so I would. Sorry, I…'

'S'alright, whatever you like.'

'Look, I don't mean to be rude but, if you don't mind me asking, who are you anyway?'

Nat stubbed out the cigarette, rose to his feet and smirked, just enough to raise one corner of his mouth. He extended his right arm as he moved towards her.

'Sorry, forgetting my manners. Nathan, Nathan Pearson. Call me Nat.'

She managed to get as far as 'pleased to…' before she froze, his words falling on her ears like lead weights. Slowly, she raised her eyes to his, her pale skin now a healthy shade of blush.

'I'm so embarrassed!' she laughed.

'My fault, I shouldn't have teased you; not fair.'

They shook hands as a matter of course but, unlike the gaze earlier, it lasted longer than was necessary. He noticed how soft and small her hands were, how comfortably they fitted his. She too was reluctant to let go.

* * *

A cacophony of conversations filled the vast dining hall that was La Coupole. As was customary, Nat was treating Jack to a celebratory dinner; probation over, she was now officially hired. Their dialogue excluded anything work-related, instead, she spoke excitedly of Paris, of her bedsit and her loathing of Kerry.

He studied her as she spoke and realised it had been four months to the day since she'd arrived on the doorstep of Citron. He looked in vain for the vulnerable, naive designer who had re-located to Paris but saw only a lass who was now virtually fluent in French, a creative with more than her fair share of talent, a young lady with the eyes of a doe and a lariat that was tightening around his heart. They were oblivious to the fact that they were holding hands across the table. It seemed the natural thing to do.

The lights dimmed as two glasses of Armagnac arrived at their table. A procession of waiters snaked their way from the kitchens towards an unsuspecting diner with a chorus of 'Bon Anniversaire', cake held aloft. It was a first for Jack, her eyes shimmered in the candlelight as she, and the hundreds of other diners, joined in the verse and applauded in unison. It was entertaining; it was tradition. Jack laughed gleefully, like a child on Christmas morning.

She smiled at Nat as if she knew him inside out, as if she'd known him from birth. He gazed back and wondered how in God's name he'd got through the last four months without a guide dog.

* * *

'Autre choses, Monsieur?' asked the waiter.

The interruption startled them, as though they had been caught in the throes of something illicit, something clandestine. They laughed at the foolishness of their own behaviour.

'No, not for me, thanks,' said Jack, 'it's late, I should go. If we're quick, I can make the Metro.'

Nat tried desperately to hide his disappointment and paid the check. He convinced himself it would never work, that it was unwise, and unprofessional, to mix business with pleasure. He escorted Jack to Vavin. They walked slowly, in silence, he with hands in pockets and gaze fixed dead ahead. He cursed himself for liking her so much.

Without warning, she whipped him round by his right arm and pulled him close. They almost fell as he lost his balance. She slid both arms up around the back of his neck and looked deep into his eyes. He stared into hers and swore he could see something burning, an inferno, something waiting to explode. She closed her eyes, raised herself up on tiptoe and kissed him softly on the lips. Naturally, he responded. The smell of her scent did something to the hairs on the back of his neck. His heart pounded. He felt like a schoolboy about to do it for the first time. He pulled her close, kissed her again and called her une pute. Their laughter echoed down the narrow street. It was like a two-piece jigsaw snapping home for the first time.

* * *

It was a virgin blade, razor-sharp and cold as steel. He felt no pain as it effortlessly, cleanly, sliced his skin. A steady trickle of crimson blood traced a lethargic route down his neck. His collar halted its progress like thirsty blotting paper.

'Merde! Fuck fuck fuck fuck fuck!'

All too late, he realised the advantage of shaving before dressing. He blamed a misty mirror and the irrepressible Johnny Halliday for the injury rather than admit to himself that he just wasn't concentrating, that his mind was elsewhere. He tousled his already unkempt hair and noticed how the crow's feet were etching ever deeper into his olive skin. He stared at his reflection and contemplated the stomach-churning reality that he would have to face Jack in the studio.

Sitting on the edge of the tub he pulled another Marlboro from his breast pocket. Drawing deeply, he considered the implications of the inevitable confrontation. He assured himself that their actions had been influenced by the copious amount of wine they had consumed and that, after all, it was only a kiss. One kiss. That was the end of it. Nonetheless, the walk to the studio was as long as a walk to the gallows. He considered a last request.

* * *

Unusual as it seemed, their paths failed to cross the entire day. Mild paranoia told him she was avoiding him but, if that was the way she wanted to play it, then fine. He'd let it go.

It was after seven when he called it a day. He needed a drink, a large one. Disappointed, and somewhat confused, he yelled a generally aimed 'à bientôt' in the direction of the studio and glanced only fleetingly at Jack.

She returned the look with the slyest of winks. It confounded him. What did that mean? Was she playing with him or was she smarter than he thought? He hit the street, not knowing whether to turn left or right, hang around or walk on. 'Fuck it' he mumbled as he drove his hands deep into his pockets and slowly walked away.

Silently and without warning, she appeared by his side, slid her arm through his and said nothing. He felt as though he was being hijacked for a second time and he didn't care where he was taken. He laughed a low, dirty laugh, as a sense of welcome relief cleansed his troubled mind. 'This,' he thought, 'is going to be bloody brilliant!'

They turned the corner into Rue Jean Bart and paused outside a bar. It was a low-brow looking place, scruffy and in need of restoration. Peeling paint hung from the timber façade, grey net curtains and dirty panes obscured the world within. A faded sign swung lazily above their heads. Nat tried the door. It opened with a creak.

'Come on, I need a drink,' he said.

* * *

The lights were dim. It was deserted; dead. Not a soul. The only sound was the drip of a beer tap and the distant tick of a clock. Jack questioned the attraction of this museum-like homage to café society. The walls, adorned with photos of Piaf's Paris, were stained yellow with nicotine. Dust lay thick on the antique chandeliers, the air was stale and the mirrors reflected a sense of doom. She was startled as Le Propriétaire rose from behind the bar and heaved a crate of 1664 onto the counter. He was tall and lean, unshaven, with long hair as black as pitch. He bit through the match hanging from the corner of his mouth and scowled at Nat with piercing blue eyes. Jack sensed a confrontation and gripped Nat's arm, instinctively taking half a step back.

'And what the fock do you want?'

The question sounded all the more threatening for his aggressive Antrim accent. Then he smiled. He smiled a smile that would have charmed the devil himself.

'Jack, this gobshite is Lennie. Gobshite, this is Jack,' said Nat.

'Hello,' she smiled, as Lennie kissed the back of her hand.

His voice was little more than a whisper.

'If I'm not mistaken, I'd say you were one of Erin's girls. Am I right?'

'Aye. Kerry,' she replied.

'Kerry, well there's a thing! Sucker for Irish eyes, me.'

'Right, you and the rest of them. So, er, how are you?'

'Me? Don't you go worrying yourself over the likes of me, now. Just remember, you're welcome here anytime, whether you're with this arse or not, got that?'

'Thanks,' she said, and walked to the back of the bar where she took a seat on a banquette.

* * *

'Done alright for yourself there, Nat, me old mate. Pretty wee thing, so she is.'

Nat smiled.

'I've got a feeling about her,' he said. 'A good feeling.'

'Is that a fact? Well, listen to your Uncle Lennie, don't you go doing anything foolish now, take it easy. I don't want to be the only bachelor left in this city. Now, I've work to do, what do you want, the plonk or the Hermitage?'

'Hermitage, let's have the Hermitage.'

Nat sat opposite Jack and lit a cigarette. She giggled as Lennie slammed two bottles of wine down on the table.

'I know this man,' he said with a wink, 'he'll not stop at one.'

* * *

They talked and laughed as the clock pulled them past midnight. He spoke of New York and Beirut, of Ben Nevis and bagels, about breathing and listening, sitting and watching. She spoke of yellow pencils, of conquering the world, of seeing and smelling and tasting and grasping everything she could lay her hands on. His words were weary with experience, hers embellished with the enthusiasm of youth.

'Show me,' she said.

'How'd you mean?'

'Take me away, show me something new.'

'Just you and me?'

'Yes.'

'Together?'

'Yes.'

'Do you know how old I am?'

'Yes!'

'That's bit forward, isn't it?'

'Christ, yes!'

He laughed, sat back and raised his glass.

'Okay then. They say travel broadens the mind.'

'And what makes you think it's my mind I want broadened?'

He spluttered as she grinned mischievously and leaned across the table to kiss him. It was a kiss that could have lasted twenty-three days had Lennie not intervened with two glasses of brandy.

'You two should be in bed by now. No! No, I mean, like, you should be... ah shite, forget it! You know what I mean. Here, lock up will you, Nat? I'm off.'

He tossed the keys on the table and slammed the door behind him. Jack smiled and cocked her head to one side.

'He's a good friend, I can tell,' she said. 'I think that's grand, to know someone like that, to have someone you can trust.'

'True. And I do... trust him, I mean.'

'Sounds serious, is there something you're not telling me?' she asked playfully.

'Oh yes,' he replied, 'loads, but listen.' He leaned forward, looked her straight in the eye and spoke softly, seriously.

'If you ever get into trouble, or you ever need anything, anything at all, you come straight here, you understand, straight here. If you can't find me, he will.'

The gravity of his remark unnerved her. She didn't know why, it just seemed odd, as though there were more to it, but she let it go and blamed the wine for her neurosis.

'Sure,' she said, 'I understand.'

Nat locked the door and pushed the keys back through the letter box. It was late, the streets were deserted and she had no doubt as to where she would be staying that night. Like postcard lovers, they walked arm in arm along the Boulevard Saint Michel saying nothing, preferring instead to savour the stillness of the night.

* * *

The sun bathed her face with the mellow light of morning. It made her smile. Eyes shut tight, she reached out to touch him, to feel his body, but he was gone. She was alone. The smile vanished and she sat bolt upright. A voice came from the hall.

'Ça-va?' he asked.

She turned to face Nat, framed by the doorway, clad in nothing but faded 501s with the mandatory Marlboro hanging from his lower lip.

'Hello. Sleep okay?'

'Yes,' she sighed, 'and you? I mean you slept right here too, didn't you...?'

'No, no, no. Out here, on the couch.'

'Out... but why? Did I...'

'No, you didn't, but I have rules about that kinda stuff, besides, we don't wanna rush things, do we? I mean, we've got the whole day, right?'

She pulled her knees to her chest and grinned inanely.

'It's late,' he said, slapping her thigh, 'you'd better get dressed or there'll be hell to pay when you hit the office. Don't wanna upset the boss now, do you?'

'Funny, hold on! What about you? Aren't you...'

'Uh-uh, got stuff to do. Tell you what though, see you back here tonight, when you're done, okay?'

'But what time, what...?'

The door closed and he was gone.

Chapter Three

'Pray love me a little, so you love me long.'

Herrick

Showered and refreshed, Nat hastened to the home of his pal and trusted mechanic, Guillaume. A week had been ample time to fit a new pair of filters and he needed his wheels back.

He and Guillaume had met through Lennie and hit it off straight away. Guillaume's Gallic arrogance was a natural foil for Nat's dry sense of humour. There was something about Guillaume that attracted women like a moth to a flame, something Nat was unable to quantify. He just couldn't figure it out. Guillaume was not good-looking; not in the conventional sense. His nose, though not large, was big – big and crooked. His eyes were close-set and his chin, pointed. Perhaps it was his ruffled, dishevelled appearance or his misogynistic attitude. Whatever it was, it wasn't just the cars he serviced on a regular basis.

* * *

Guillaume opened the door in a state of bewildered undress, his brylcreemed hair slicked back, his brow furrowed.

'Huh? Nathan! Non, non, non! Now is not a good time, ami, I have a… a friend, visiting, a sick friend!'

'D'accord, Guillaume, d'accord,' said Nat. 'Une amie nommé désire, non?'

'Ha, ha, ha, trés amusant, ros-bif, trés amusant. Look, I am laughing. Alors, venez, venez, mais restez-pas, okay? Please, Nathan, you do not stay, okay?'

'Sure, man, sure, sure, I just came for the bike, that's all. You have done it, haven't you?'

'Yes, yes, all finished; she purrs, like a cat!'

They entered the apartment and Nat took a seat while Guillaume frantically changed into something suitable for the street.

A young lady called from the bathroom: 'Cuckoo! Cuckoo!' Nat said nothing. A wry grin crept across his face. Again, she called, this time, louder. 'Cuckoo! Cuckoo!' The door flew open and the young lady bounded into the room wearing nothing but a baseball cap and motorcycle boots.

'Va-voom!' she cried 'Regardez-moi! Je veux aller faire un tour!'

She froze as her eyes met Nat's.

'Moi aussi,' he quipped. 'Moi aussi'.

'Aiiiiieeeee! Guillaume, c'est pas un cabaret!' she screamed and ran to the bathroom.

Guillaume dashed from the bedroom, concerned at the commotion.

'Qu'est-ce qu'il y a?' he yelled.

'Rien,' said Nat. 'Une autre motocycliste, c'est tout.'

'Ah, Nathan, that does it! You must get the bike yourself, you are upsetting my guest! Don't you see how ill she is!'

He threw him the keys and ran to his pillion.

* * *

The pulsating grunt of the exhaust reverberated off the garage door. The sound was low and healthy, a rhythmic duh, duh, duh, which threatened to trigger every car alarm in the vicinity. With a flick of his foot, it clunked satisfyingly into first. He dropped the clutch and grinned maniacally as the front wheel parted company with the tarmac. As usual, Guillaume had tuned it to perfection; it pulled like a crane with every blip of the throttle.

Buzzing around the Parisian streets was a pastime he relished for all the wrong reasons. He enjoyed the fact that every trip was fraught with danger. That most drivers had little or no regard for other road users. That even more failed to notice their cars were equipped with minor extras like rear-view mirrors and indicators.

After nineteen miles on a trip to nowhere he slalomed his way to the poissonnerie on the Rue St. Antoine and was relieved to find it bereft of the usual bored housewives who did little more than moan about the state of their plumbing, their husbands' plumbing or the mangy stray they'd taken in.

He filled his lungs with the smell of the ocean and was sorely tempted to visit the bouchèrie instead. He endured the odour only as long as was necessary to procure two large tuna steaks. He knew Jack liked fish. He would cook. It would be a surprise. A nice surprise, he hoped. Two stores down and, more importantly, he procured the main ingredient – two bottles of Margaux, 1986, and charged them to his card without a thought.

* * *

The apartment was uncomfortably warm, almost muggy. He threw open the windows and allowed what little breeze there was to permeate the room. The humid air told him there was a storm brewing. He tossed the steaks in a pan, filled a beaker with wine, sat in the window and waited. The world raced home beneath him. Heavy spots of rain splashed sporadically on the sill. The buzzer sounded on the stroke of seven.

'Oui?' he drawled.

'Hi! It's me, Jack!'

'Allo? Qui là?'

'It's me, Jack!'

'Jacques?'

'Oh, for Christ's sake, open the fu...'

He listened as she clumped wearily up the stairs. The door opened and she appeared, feigning a look of utter contempt. It was not an Oscar winning performance. Nat smiled.

'You should've taken the lift.'

'Lift? I didn't know there was a...'

She rolled her eyes, kicked off her shoes and slumped on the couch. He handed her a glass of wine. It was the only glass in the apartment and now it was hers. She took a large swig and sighed with relief. It was just the fillip she needed after a day that had lasted nine hours too long.

She closed her eyes and relaxed. Nathan couldn't help but notice how small and vulnerable she looked on the over-sized sofa; how the milky-white inch or two of naked thigh contrasted sharply with the black of her stockings and skirt.

She opened her eyes and caught him staring.

'And what do you think you're looking at, Mister?' she said.

He paused before answering.

'My future,' he said, and repaired to the kitchen.

Nat raised his beaker.

'Bon appetite,' he said. 'Hope you like it.'

She took a mouthful.

'This…' she said between mouthfuls 'is feckin' gorgeous! Do you have anything to go with it? Any vegetables maybe? Or some rice?'

'Eh?'

'That'll be a no then.'

'Shit. Sorry, I knew there was something. Got some Dijon. Any good?'

'No worries, I'll stick with the wine. Mmm. Margaux, I reckon.'

'Margaux? How the hell do you know it's Margaux?'

'Not just a pretty face from Bogland, you know. Saw the label, so I did.'

They moved to the couch with the last bottle of wine. She sat with her head on his shoulder, legs pulled up beneath her. They said nothing but listened instead to Dolores O'Riordon drifting from the battered transistor radio:

I know I've felt like this before,
but now I'm feeling it even more,
because it came from you…
And now I tell you openly,

you have my heart so don't hurt me,
you're what I couldn't find.
Talk to me amazing mind,
so understanding and so kind,
you're everything to me.

* * *

They were weary in a way that came from doing nothing; from sitting and eating and from drinking too much wine. She beckoned him to bed. Their clothes fell to the floor and they slid beneath the cool cotton sheets. They lay side by side and stared intently at each other, noting every line, every crease, every wrinkle. A static charge shocked their lips as they kissed. She arched her back as he stroked her breast for the first time. Three hours later they collapsed in love.

* * *

'So this is Armageddon,' he thought.

Claps of thunder exploded overhead and rumbled down the narrow street below. He sat, naked, in the window and counted. The lightning flashed, illuminating marshmallow clouds in a blaze of technicolour brilliance. He counted.

'One...'

The next clap almost shook him from his perch. A pall of blue-tinged smoke hung in the air as the lightning flashed again. He could sense Jack's presence and spoke without turning round.

'Take a look, Jack, it's unbelievable. Beautiful. Just beautiful.'

'The Gods are angry, that's for sure,' she whispered as she slid her arms around his shoulders.

'You've a thing for water, don't you Nat?'

'Eh?'

'You. You and water. You stare at the river; you walk in the rain. Bet you're a Pisces.'

'Nope. Tiger. Or cheetah or something.'

'Didn't know you liked Chinese.'

'I don't, not really, but I believe in the cycle.'

'What cycle?'

He turned to face her. Dappled moonlight shimmered on his greying stubble.

'Samsara. The here and now. It's a temporary phase. We're just passing through.'

'You mean reincarnation?'

'If you like.'

'And how will you know?'

'Because I believe.'

'And how will I know?'

'You'll know. Trust me. You'll know.'

Chapter Four

'Keep your fears to yourself,
but share your courage.'

Duke of Wellington

A crisp, light breeze blew through the window and sent a shiver down her spine. The storm had passed. Small white clouds drifted in its wake. Nat called from the kitchen.

'Ten minutes,' he yelled.

She grimaced and showered briskly.

'I've nothing to wear!' she said, shivering in a towel.

He handed her a tee-shirt and a turtleneck sweater.

'Course you have,' he said.

She stared blankly.

'They'll talk,' she said.

'Who?'

'The girls of course!'

'Does it matter?'

'Well, I...'

'Come on, chop, chop, we need to go.'

She pulled the sweater over her head and breathed deeply. The smell excited her. She smiled. She couldn't wait to see the girls. Nat passed her a crash helmet.

'If it feels loose, strap it tight,' he said. 'We'll get you a proper one later.'

It was her first time on a bike. It was a baptism of fire. Fuelled by fear, she grabbed his waist and hollered with delight as the front wheel made forty degrees with the tarmac. Barely pausing at the junction, he sped across the Rue St. Antoine and raced the wrong way up Rue Fr. Miron before crossing the Seine under the watchful eye of Notre Dame. Seven minutes later, they arrived at the office.

Jack leapt from the bike, grabbed him by the collar with both hands and kissed him. Hard. She pouted and ran upstairs. Nat followed. They were greeted, somewhat predictably, with a mixture of dropped-jaws and raised eyebrows. The questions came thick and fast.

'Je suis fou de quelqu'un, c'est tout. Fou!' was all she said.

Her level of concentration peaked at zero for the entire morning. She declined the offer of lunch with inquisitive colleagues; if they want gossip, they can read *Hello*. Instead she rapped the door of Nat's office and walked in.

He was staring at the Mac.

'What's up?' he asked.

'Nothing. Bored. Hungry,' she said. 'You?'

He sat back and smiled.

'Same,' he said. 'Some clients I can do without. Come on, let's walk.'

* * *

27

They sauntered towards Montparnasse, ambling like tourists killing time in a strange city and stopped, momentarily, to browse the window of the agence immobilière. Blurred photos of tiny apartments made him sigh. Then, together, they pointed at a small snap of a run-down château in the Normandy countryside. It was in need of restoration. They looked at each other and smiled.

'What do you see?' asked Nat.

She stared at photo.

'Apple trees. An orchard. Wild roses. Chickens – bantams running free.'

'That it?'

'For now. What do you see?' she asked.

'I see an open fire. And a dog. And happy. I see happy.'

He didn't see what was coming next.

* * *

Nat reclined with a Marlboro. He derived a strange satisfaction from refusing work. He was now one client down but it was a weight off his shoulders. He contemplated the evening ahead: beer or wine? Wine or beer? It was a tough choice, and one he didn't have to make. The phone rang. He picked up on the third ring. There was a slight pause. A gravelly voice spoke slowly.

'It's carnival time. Buy a mask.'

He stood abruptly.

'Eh? Quittez-pas!'

The line went dead.

'Don't hang up!' he yelled.

He slammed the phone down. His pulse raced; tiny beads of perspiration gathered on his forehead. He sat, bewildered, wide-eyed in disbelief. He stood, he paced the room, he sat down again. He stared at the phone and cursed profusely.

'Not now!' he grumbled under his breath. 'Why the fuck now? Three years, nothing! And now – now? Here we go, oh, here we fuckin' go!'

He took a deep breath and opened the safe in the corner of the office. He pulled the contents to the floor: piles of documents, spent cheque-books and the petty cash, and fumbled for the jiffy bag nestling at the back. Using a handkerchief, he removed the contents, wiped away the oil and stared at the Glock in disbelief. Mumbling like a madman, he loaded the clip, stuffed the surplus rounds in his pocket and rammed everything back in the safe. There was no time for deliberation, he had to move fast. This was a part of his life he wished to forget, a side to him he wanted no-one to see, one contract he wished he'd refused.

The gun hung heavy in his jacket pocket. He grabbed his helmet and stopped at the front desk where he instructed the receptionist to use her initiative in fending off any calls and sent for Jack. She appeared in the lobby, smiling. Nat was not.

'Listen, Jack, I've gotta go, can't explain, I'll see ya later, okay?'

'Sure, your place tonight...' she whispered with a grin.

'No! Listen! I will call. Now, trust me.'

He pulled her close and hugged her tightly.

'You're scaring me.'

'Trust me. And remember the bar. Lennie's. Yes?' He gripped her by the shoulders. 'Trust me. I love you.'

Three little words, just three little words obliterated everything she'd just felt beforehand. Her eyes glazed over.

'I love you too,' she said.

* * *

Within a second he was gone. The noise from the street drew the staff to the window. They got there just in time to catch a glimpse of Nat as he sped down the road, wrestling with the bike as the rubber fought to get a grip on the tarmac. Jack choked as she recalled the gravity of what he'd said and Nat swore as his bowels threatened to empty at any moment.

The ride to Neufchâtel did not take long. The sleepy, picturesque village did not have much: one road, two hotels, five bars and a reputation for cheese. Not, he thought, the ideal place for an under-cover rendez-vous but he could do worse. He checked into the Hôtel Le Grand Cerf, not knowing if he would stay the night.

He sat in darkness, three feet from the window and waited. And waited. And waited. He muttered to himself:

'A last request, monsieur?'

'Fromage! Fromage de Neufchâtel!'

The bar was one flight down. It was tempting. One drop and he'd have to quit. One drop and he could leave. Finally, the phone rang. It was 11pm. Nat picked up on the first ring. He listened, replaced the receiver and flicked the catch off the Glock. From the shadows of the lobby, he watched as a priest in a flowing cassock and pill-box hat hastened across the courtyard and entered the church. He waited sixty seconds and followed.

The church was dark. Black. 'Black as Satan's asshole.' He waited for his eyes to dilate. A handful of scented candles flickered nervously, the air was musty and damp. Halfway up the aisle sat the figure in the pill-box hat. Nat slid silently into the pew behind him.

'Okay, you got me here. What's up?' he whispered.

Silence. He leaned forward, asked again and jabbed the priest sharply in the shoulder. He slumped forward. The crack of his head as it hit the pew echoed throughout the church. Nat dropped to his knees and froze. He pulled the pistol from his pocket and listened. The only sound was that of his heart, pounding in his ears. The minutes passed slowly until, confident he was alone, he rose to take a closer look at the corpse. He pulled him upright and squatted beside him. The Zippo clunked open. Nat stared by the light of the flame. He wasn't European. He looked Latino. Colombian maybe. He had a face like a pickle and smelled like a goat.

Nat lit a Marlboro, inhaled deeply and sighed: 'So, who the fuck are you?'

'He'll not be one of us, that's for sure.'

Quick as a flash, he spun on his heels as Lennie, complete with dog collar, stepped from the shadows. Nat lowered the gun.

'One day, I swear, one day you're gonna give me a cardiac. You look more like a priest than a fuckin' priest.'

'Less of the blaspheming my child, you're in a holy place now, so you are.'

'Holy place my ass, he's the one with the hole in him. Your handiwork?'

''Fraid so. Had no choice. For a start, I didn't invite him, and secondly, he'd have put you away without so much as a Hail Mary. Now, c'mon, I've news for you and you're not going to like it.'

* * *

They went to the vestry and gently closed the door behind them.

Nat surveyed his surroundings, the opulent furnishings and crates of wine, with a cynical eye. The Catholic church, so far as he was concerned, was nothing more than a temple of hypocrisy. Lennie paced the floor. He seemed frustrated; agitated. It was out of character. Nat had witnessed this behaviour before. Just once. He swallowed and braced himself for the bad news about to break. Lennie stopped in his tracks and turned to Nat, hands clasped tight beneath his chin.

'You've a good memory, so you have. Remember how this started?'

'You mean Bologna? Cosmoprof, right?'

Chapter Five

*'God put me on earth to accomplish
a certain number of things.
Right now, I am so far behind,
I will never die.'*

Calvin and Hobbes

The heat was uncomfortable, ninety degrees and climbing.
His knees were weak. The Tuscan hillsides shimmered in
the distance and the terracotta rooftops glowed with
shades of burnt sienna. The view was nothing less than
stunning, his standpoint nothing more than an exercise in
stupidity.

Having conquered the impossibly steep, narrow
stairway to the roof, he stood with his back to the wall and
watched as the dome of Il Duomo fell away beneath him,
taking with it every drop of machismo in his body. There
was no rational explanation for this sudden attack of
vertigo, other than he hadn't eaten in twelve hours and had

stood for the duration of the train journey from Milan. It was time to get off the carrousel.

The temperature at street level was more agreeable and the ground didn't seem to spin as much. It was two-thirty, which afforded Nat ample time for lunch before his meeting at the Hotel Mario with Susie Hernandez.

With Susie he had enjoyed a profitable, working relationship for nearly two years. She owned a small, but successful, cosmetics company called Suzie-Q and he had been responsible for designing the brand and its components. They would travel together, the following day, to the annual international trade fair known as Cosmoprof, held in Bologna.

Nat took a table outside Osteria in the Piazza Santo Spirito and watched the locals plod about their carefree existence. The men dressed identically – loafers (no socks), chinos and a polo shirt with, despite the heat, a sweater tied neatly across the shoulders. The women wore Chanel. Their skirts were short; legs bronzed. They hid behind their Wayfarers.

A waiter brought Nat a large Chianti, some bread and olive oil. An hour became two, then three. The low evening sun begged him to stay. The Chianti told him to go.

* * *

The name of the hotel had three crowns painted above it. They meant nothing. From the street it looked decidedly average. Inside was not much better but it was clean and comfortable in a traditional, homely way. He checked in and smirked as the blushing receptionist pointed him the direction of his room.

He showered, changed and made his way to the bar where he sipped a sublime Tanqueray and tonic. The worn Chesterfield felt like an old friend, one with whom he had to part, as Susie blew through the door. It was enough to prompt another Marlboro.

'Nathan! Oooh-hoo! Nathan, honey! Buongiorno, baby!' she hollered.

He masked his disdain for the forced mid-Atlantic accent and mustered a genuine smile. She was okay – a little brash, more broad than dame – but she was okay. Her heart was in the right place.

'Susie! How are you? Need a drink?'

'Oh, do I? Martini, darling; dry, no olive. What's with this place? We slumming it?'

She squeezed next to Nat and adjusted her ample bosom as the drinks arrived. She glanced up as she sipped her Martini, crossed her long, orange legs and opened her filofax.

'Now then Nat, Nathan, honey,' she said, licking the tip of her index finger, 'we have a big day tomorrow; I mean big. People to see, things to do, we should have a schedule.'

'Oh, Susie, please, no. No schedule. It's been a long day, let's just see what happens, eh? Okay? Let's just have a coupla drinks and something to eat.'

She closed her book, turned to Nat and picked imaginary bits of fluff off his shoulder.

'Why, Nathan Pearson, are you asking me to dinner?' she purred.

'Huh? Ah, Susie, stop flirting, will ya? You wanna eat or what?'

'Sure, spoilsport, sure, let's eat.'

* * *

They crossed the Ponte Vecchio as a golden sun sank slowly into slumber. Susie picked a restaurant, upmarket, with chandeliers and waiters in tail-coats. They were led to a table slightly more intimate than cosy. Susie giggled as the wine flowed.

'Nathan, dearest, before I forget, tomorrow you're gonna meet Ramon, my Ramon. You two have never met, have you?'

'Nope, can't say we...'

'No matter. I've told him all about you and he figures you could maybe work together. How about that!'

'Excuse me? Work? Like how?'

'He has a project, don't ask, I don't know. Anyhow, he needs a designer, he's seen your stuff so he figures, hey, he's a designer, let's talk.'

'Cool. I think. Thanks Susie, appreciate it.'

'Whatever.'

He felt a stockinged foot run up his calf and along his thigh. It was time to leave. They strolled back to the hotel, Nat, like a doting husband, has his arm around her shoulder. Without it, gravity would pull her to the ground.

He took Susie to her room, opened the door and leant her against the wall. He spoke like an adult chastising his youngest.

'Get some sleep and remember the train leaves at eight sharp. See you over coffee at seven, you got that? Seven!'

'Got it,' she slurred, as she lunged and stole a kiss.

* * *

Nat was waiting. She appeared, looking impossibly fresh, downed his coffee and beckoned him to the door.

'Come on! We have a train to catch!'

Cosmoprof was into its second day. Nat yawned. It had the same effect as a bottle of sleeping pills. Geared around and for the cosmetics, fragrance and toiletry industries, it comprised the usual medley of manufacturers and suppliers plying their wares. It was a showcase for new technology and an opportunity for the exhibitors to sign some lucrative new contracts. Everything was available from heavy-duty on-line packing machinery to brand new products for the professional and retail markets. Nat yawned again. He wondered if he was narcoleptic. Things were getting worse, the crowds were swelling and it annoyed him. If there were two things in life he tried to avoid, they were crowds and noise.

Susie's screams grated on his fillings.

'Ramon! Ray, honey! Over here!' she screeched, waving her arms like a windmill on crack. 'Ramon, there you are! This is him! This is Nathan, the designer guy! Nat, this is my husband, Ramon.'

* * *

They made the most unlikely looking pair he'd ever seen. Ramon Hernandez was a big man, six-feet, four and a half inches tall, two-hundred and sixty pounds, and virtually bald. He looked the bad side of sixty and had a complexion like lumpy guacamole.

Either he owns Colombia, thought Nat, or he's hung like a mule.

They shook hands and exchanged pleasantries.

'So, Pearson, how about a drink?'

'The names Nat, Fernandez, Nat.'

'It's Hernandez!'

'Whatever.'

'Point taken Mr Pearson, I mean, Nat. I'm glad to see I am dealing with someone of substance. Most people feel intimidated by me.'

'Must be your size.'

'Pardon me?'

'Not very wise. How about that drink?'

They sat at a bar where the crowds were thinner and the noise level more conducive to conversation. The South American ordered two large brandies, their conversation was brief.

'So,' began Hernandez. 'I have seen your work, I am impressed. Susannah says you have worked for some big houses too.'

'A couple,' said Nat, 'Givenchy, Patou. I get by.'

'That, my friend, is good enough for me. Salud!'

He downed the brandy and stood to leave.

'We must talk business,' he continued. 'Tonight?'

'Sure, sure, what d'ya have in mind?'

'Dinner. Here take this, it has the name and the address of the restaurant on it. Shall we say eight o'clock?'

* * *

The restaurant was a haven for clandestine meetings. Located in a quiet side-street, its sombre appearance belied the activity inside. It was full of transients, couples, backpackers and misfits who neither cared for, nor were interested in the other diners.

Weaving his way through the diners, he squeezed by a group of six men sat in row at a long table. They were talking Italian, wore skinny black ties and had their shirt sleeves rolled neatly to just above the elbow. All had receding hair-lines and they ate with their hands. Their conversation stopped as he passed them by, six pairs of eyes tracked his every move.

Long way from Palermo, thought Nat. Susie called him to the table.

Hernandez remained seated. The wall lamp directly above his head cast a sinister shadow across his face. He looked menacing and a great deal older than Nat recalled. A glass was charged in anticipation of his arrival.

'Don't get up,' he said as he took a seat.

Hernandez glared.

'First we talk, then we eat,' he said.

* * *

Nat listened intently as Ramon divulged the background to the project. It was nothing less than remarkable, nothing more than ambitious.

'I have a company, a big company. Rio Logica. We have a vested interest in the Soviet Union, or should I say, the free markets of the independent Soviet states. In other words, the barriers are down. It is time to capitalise on that. It's time to trade and I intend to trade. I intend to profit. People are curious to know what has been going on in a country that has hidden its interests from the west for a hundred years.'

'Okay, I...'

'Moldavia. That is where my interest lies. No longer tied to the Draconian ways of the old regime it considers itself European. It wants to move forward, distance itself from the USSR and enjoy the spoils of a capitalist economy.'

Nat sipped his wine.

'Go on,' he said.

'I am going to help them achieve their goal. I am going to open them up to the commercial profiteering and underhand dealing that we as westerners have grown to love. I have met with the president regarding this... investment. I have also met with his "advisors", those in charge of industry. You understand what I mean?'

'You mean they're all on the payroll. Kinda like democracy, but not as we know it.'

'The president lives in splendour; the populace live on vegetables. You could call it a dictatorship. Many have. Unfortunately, all that remains of them now is a simple epitaph. It does not bother me, I can work with people like this. The question is: can you work with someone like me?'

Nat hesitated and reached for a Marlboro.

'Don't be alarmed!' said Hernandez. 'It's just you and me, simply a business deal. You can write your own epitaph. It's a joke, I made a joke!'

Nat was not amused. He glanced at Susie, looking for some kind of reassurance. There was none. She was completely, totally and unashamedly bored. Her husband continued.

'Let me get to the point. The point is why do I need you? Simple. We have developed a fragrance, a perfume, with a little help of course. You look surprised, you imagine, perhaps, this is strange?'

'No, no, I just thought, cars maybe, or electronics, grain...'

'Too obvious, that's why this is brilliant. Listen, in a matter of weeks we shall be opening a plant a few kilometres outside Kishinev. This is where the fragrance will be produced. It will be the first product of its kind, the first quality product to ever be exported from the East to the West. Think about it, who ever heard of a perfume from Russia? Italy, yes. France, yes. Beverly Hills, of course! But Russia? Moldovia? And that's not all; no, no. Each bottle will contain gold, real gold, floating in the liquid. They will be clamouring to buy it.'

'Maybe.'

'Maybe? You want to know why "maybe" doesn't matter? I'll tell you: profit. The perfume will cost almost nothing to produce. The retail will be around, let's say, three hundred dollars. It will be hailed as a benchmark for the future of free enterprise in East-West relationships.'

'Okay, well, what do you want? I'm kinda hungry,' said Nat.

Hernandez paused deliberately before continuing.

'The task, for someone of your calibre, is very simple. I need a name for the perfume, plus a bottle and a carton. There are only two restrictions. One: we have only eight weeks, so no research and no trials. On this, I must insist. Two: the bottle will be made in crystal, lead crystal. To justify the... er... re-sale value, you understand?'

'We make the bottles here and ship them to Kishinev?'

'Yes. So, what do you say? Can you do it?'

'Sure. I can do it. All I need to know is, how much juice is this bottle gonna hold and... how much are you gonna pay me.'

'One point five fluid ounces. Five hundred thousand US dollars.'

Nat glanced at Susie. She raised her left eyebrow and winked.

'I guess that's okay,' he said.

'Excellent! Now, we eat!'

Chapter Six

*'Everyone is as God made him
and often a great deal worse.'*

Cervantes

It was early. The sparrows chirped as the city slept. It was his time of day. That brief couple of hours when the sky changed from a dark, motley grey to a pale blue. When the streetlamps went to sleep. When the sound of a solitary dustcart was almost poetic.

The match crackled and fizzed as Nat sparked another Marlboro and stared proudly at the concepts. He was a happy man. Three designs, three names, three prototypes, but it was 'Zhar-ptitsa' that stood out. 'The Firebird'. It had the creativity of Dhiagilev. The sensitivity of Stravinsky's score. It was modern and bold, yet delicate and understated. It was classy. In forty-eight hours, he would either be fêted or exiled to the Gulag.

Nat grabbed the mail from the lobby, tossed the circulars and bills on the receptionist's desk and took the remaining two envelopes to his office. The first contained his travel documents: Aeroflot to Kiev, via Moscow, and transfer by rail to Kishinev. The second was addressed to him personally and carried a postmark from Bern. There was no correspondence, just a banker's draft made payable to 'Citron S.A.' for the sum of five hundred thousand US dollars. He laughed out loud and left it on his secretary's desk with a large Post-it Note instructing her to bank it before she even took her coat off.

Back in his office, he settled down with a cup of coffee and *Le Monde*. The phone rang as he turned to page three. It was Susie, distraught, distressed, upset and on her way over. He hoped it wasn't serious.

He prised his mug from the paper to reveal three inches of column space given to a story intriguing by its lack of detail: 'MEUTRE A BOU' HAUSSMANN'. 'The body of Monsieur R. Hernandez was discovered in his apartment in the early hours of the morning.'

'Fuck!'

He waited in the lobby for Susie to arrive, concerned now for her welfare. He wondered, briefly, if the project was now in jeopardy. He drew heavily on his cigarette and assumed Susie had already been interviewed by the police; in fact, he assumed it was she who had discovered the body. He assumed wrong.

He watched in dismay as her car slew to a halt, accompanied by the sound of screeching brakes. The Carrera suited her style, the head-scarf and shades did not. They were pure Hepburn, she was more Monroe. They embraced briefly. She insisted on walking down the street rather than sitting in Nat's office. Strangely, thought Nat, she was neither upset nor angry. Worryingly, she was scared, on edge, nervous. She clutched his arm and cast backward glances over her shoulder. She had little to say. She too, had learned of her husband's demise in the paper and, for reasons of her own, did want to be entertained by the Sûreté. She hadn't seen Ramon in two days and hadn't even been to their apartment. She was leaving for Switzerland. The postmark on the envelope flashed through his mind. Bern. He could make sense of none of it. They walked to her car and stood in the light drizzle as she said her farewells.

'Thanks, Nathan – for everything. I'll be in touch. Soon. I'm sorry, I didn't know about it. Really, I...'

'About what...?'

The door slammed and she sped towards the Boulevard Montparnasse leaving Nat in a state of complete and utter confusion.

It was a little before nine and the urge to take a drink was almost overwhelming. He went back to the office and pulled the stopper from a bottle of Jack.

* * *

'Dare say you'll be needing that.'

Nat spun around, taken totally by surprise and stared at the lanky figure standing behind the door. He was tall with unruly hair and three days' growth on his chin. His raincoat hung loosely on his shoulders and his hands remained firmly in his pockets.

'Who the fuck are you?' snapped Nat, gripping the bottle by the neck.

'Whoa! Easy, mister, I just need a wee chat, that's all.'

'I'm warning you, if you… hold on. What the fuck is an Irishman doing…'

Nat stopped as the man produced his ID.

'Cashel. Lennie Cashel. Interpol.'

'Interpol? Ah.'

Nat sat down, replaced the stopper and stared at Cashel.

'Hernandez, right? So, what's up, Antrim, think I did it?' he said.

'Antrim, that's good. I heard you were good.'

'What do you mean, good?'

'No matter. I know everything about you, Mr Pearson...' He paused. 'Sergeant Pearson.'

'Sergeant? That was a long… Look, what the fuck do I know? Shouldn't you be talking to his wife?'

'Oh we will, right enough. Soon as she's off the plane. But now, just now, I need a wee talk with yourself.'

Nat drew a breath and calmed down.

'Okay. Okay. So, what d'you wanna know?'

'Hernandez. Everything. And anything.'

'Not much to tell, really. Only met a few weeks back, Susie introdu...'

'I know.'

'How do you…?'

'Tell me about the project you've been working on.'

'Project? Christ! How on earth do you know about the…?'

He waved his hand over the desk.

'What the fuck. It's all here, take a look.'

* * *

The following morning Nat was summoned to meet Cashel at the commissariat on Rue Jules Breton and was shown immediately to an interview room. One desk, two chairs. What light there was crept in through a window twelve feet from the ground. It had the ambience of a mental institution. He lit a cigarette.

Cashel breezed in, another day's growth and bags under his eyes. He sat across the table from Nat and rubbed his chin as though it might alleviate his anxieties.

'Thanks for coming, Nat. How's yourself?'

'Better than you by the looks of it.'

'Ha! I don't doubt that, not for a minute. So, tell me, has anyone been in touch, about the project?'

'Nope. No-one. But then, why should they?'

'Cancel the project, maybe? Give you a new contact? Who knows, either way, I thought they'd move quicker than this, so I did.'

'They? What're you driving at?'

Lennie leant back in his chair, scratched his head with both hands and took a deep breath.

'Okay, I'm taking you into my confidence here. Not a word, right? There's some stuff you should know about Ramon Hernandez.'

'Go on.'

'Rio Logica. It's a pharmaceutical company; don't look surprised, it knocks out aspirin, little more. It's basically a front, a cover, for a whole heap of shite. Cocaine from Colombia, hashish from Turkey, diamonds from South Africa…'

'You are ki…'

'I kid you not. He's a clever man…'

'He's a dead man.'

'He's a clever man. We've been on his tail for years but just can't pin him down. This project could be the break we've been looking for. Gold. That's the key here. It's something to do with the gold.'

'No way! I mean, you won't get rich on the gold in the juice, it's less than...'

'Trust me on this. He talked to you about the launch, in the States, right?'

'Yeah, New York.'

'Makes sense. Did he mention who was handling things that end?'

'No.'

'Well it's a fella called Kowolski. Bullion dealer. A nastier man, you will never meet. Pure evil.'

Nat stubbed out the cigarette and looked pensively at Cashel.

'So, where's this leading?'

'I need your help. If we pull it off, drinks on me. If we don't…'

'If we don't?'

'If we don't, I'll have to talk to your next of kin. If you want to walk away, that's fine. I understand. Only thing is, you don't have time to think about it.'

Nat stood and gazed up at the window, hands clasped behind his back. The sunlight streamed across his face as he chewed his lower lip. He wasn't one for procrastination.

'Okay,' he said, 'I'm in. What's next?'

Cashel slapped him on the shoulder. It was gratitude enough.

'Good man. Okay. All you have to do for now is keep the meeting as planned. Someone'll replace Hernandez and my guess is you won't know who until you get there. One thing, you'll have to wear a wire. Don't worry, we'll be right behind you. Just don't let them see it.'

'And if they do?'

'You're on your own.'

* * *

Flight SU254 was not one of Aeroflot's most popular routes. He took his seat in row two, by the window, and buckled up in preparation for take-off. A leggy stewardess brought him a newspaper and a Bloody Mary. Behind him sat Cashel, already dozing. Four tedious hours later they touched down at Moscow Sheremetyevo. Nat pulled his case from the overhead locker. Cashel was nowhere to be seen.

The repetitive questioning by immigration was loaded with aggression, pushing Nat's patience to the brink. Eventually, almost reluctantly, they waved him through and he went in search of his connecting flight. Vigilant as ever, he watched for Cashel and his entourage but could see them nowhere. This was reassuring, for if he could spot them, anyone could.

Though the trip to Kiev was a painless sixty-minute hop, he was dismayed to discover the two hundred miles or so to Kishinev would take ten hours. The train swung from side to side as it rattled lethargically through the bleak landscape. There was little to do except wander back and forth between his seat and the restaurant car and stare out of the window. The train juddered to a halt. It was not the Kishinev he expected. It was 1917.

He stood under the arches at the front of the station and waited. Two Marlboros later, a taxi arrived. He handed the driver a piece of paper and clambered in the back. The jalopy coughed and spluttered its way toward the Hotel Europe. It was a modest affair, small, the epitome of no-star accommodation. The clerk took great delight in answering the phone in both Russian and English: 'Thank you for calling me Hotel Europe, I am helping you now?'

The room, twelve feet square, was painted battleship grey. A naked bulb hung from the centre of the ceiling. A solitary can of Coke sat in the minibar. Solzhenitsyn would have felt at home.

He freshened up, went to the bar and ordered a gin. He was given the bottle, Gordon's, and a glass. He dined alone. Rabbit and potato stew. It wasn't fresh but it did stay down. He took the bottle and went to bed.

Strada Vasile Alecsandri was a twenty-minute stroll from the hotel. Trees lined the street, the traffic was light and the buildings an eclectic mix of shops and residences, all dated back to the 1950s. All except the imposing offices of Rio Logica. It towered above its surroundings with a brash modernity. It was white, imposing and clinical. The tall, perimeter fence, tinted windows and armed security guards lent an air of hostility.

A guard pointed him towards reception where he announced his appointment with Hernandez. From there he was escorted to a plush, though sparsely, furnished room. A portrait of Gorbachev hung on the wall, flanked by Lenin and Stalin. It was clear that whoever occupied the office was a very confused individual.

A small, balding man strode purposefully into the room. He was swathed in an over-sized, navy-blue Versace suit and wore fashionably round, wire spectacles. He proffered both hands as he greeted Nat with the keenest of smiles. His rotting teeth looked as though they'd been ground flat with a file and suggested his roots were humbler than his present circumstances. There was something sinister about him, something devious, something very Peter Lorre.

'Dinikin. Valery Dinikin,' he said. 'So very good to meet you, Mr Pearson.'

His voice whined like a power-drill on the slowest setting.

'Likewise, I'm sure,' replied Nat.

'You have had a good journey, yes? Enjoying your visit? Good! Most excellent! Please, sit!'

'Thank you,' said Nat. 'Thank you very much.'

'So! Down to business...'

Nat hesitated.

'Oh, what about Ramon? Shouldn't we wait for Señor Hernandez?'

Dinikin sighed and scratched the side of his face.

'That would be a very long wait, my friend. I'm afraid Señor Hernandez is, er, he is no longer with us.'

'No longer...? You mean he quit?'

'In a manner of speaking. Heart attack.'

'Huh?'

'His heart stopped working. He's dead.' Dinikin grinned. 'Look, one tiny heart trying to pump blood around that huge body. It was inevitable.'

Nat feigned surprise.

'But I just saw him, I mean a few weeks... sorry, bit of a shock.'

'When the reaper calls, Mr Pearson, he doesn't make an appointment.'

'How right you are. What about the... I mean, the project... is it still...?'

'Of course! It is very exciting, no? I am in charge now. Come, show me, we'll use my desk.'

* * *

Nat began his presentation. Dinikin, who knew little about fragrance and less about the market, was engrossed in the removal of dirt from beneath his fingernails. Nat kept it short and sweet, shoved two of the concepts back in the folio, and showed him the 'Firebird'.

'The Firebird! Brilliant! You have done your homework, Mr Pearson. I congratulate you on your, er, creativity.'

'Thank you. Now, I expect you'll want to make some changes. Colours maybe, choice of…'

'Changes? But it is beautiful as it is. No changes.'

'Are you sure? I mean…'

'Nothing. We will go with it exactly as it is. We have deadlines, Mr Pearson. So, your move. What happens next?'

'Well, let's see, we have to produce artwork for the logo and the coffret, then get proofs for your approval. We'll have to get moulds for the bottle, then there's the boring stuff – we'll need purchase orders, quantities, shipping address…'

'You have much to do, don't let me hold you up. Leave a list of what you need and I'll have the information sent to your office. It will be waiting for you by the time you return to Paris. Now, you really must excuse me, but with Hernandez out of the wa… I mean, no longer with us, I have much to do.'

* * *

Meeting over, Nat returned to the hotel and packed. He pondered events as the taxi trundled to the station. Cashel was right, there was no genuine interest in Firebird as a commercial venture, no interest at all.

Nat was last to disembark. The trip home had left him tired, hungry and in need of a shower. He wearily trudged towards passport control where he saw Lennie waiting with an immigration officer. He waved him over.

'Put it away, you'll not need that,' said Cashel, pointing at his passport. 'Top man, so you are, good job!'

Nat smiled.

'Ta. So, what d'you think? Did you get it?'

'We got it all. C'mon, we'll talk later; I've a car out front, I'll give you a ride. You can lose the wire now.'

* * *

It was still dark when Nat arrived at the studio. He made himself a coffee, went to the office and ripped a fax from the machine. Dinikin, if nothing else, had kept his word. There were the specs for the decanter, quantities and delivery addresses, details of the carton manufacturer and printer in Kishinev, contact names, telephone numbers and even the necessary purchase orders. Dinikin was acting with Germanic efficiency.

Nat was about to call the bottle manufacturers, Verreries Duvalle, in Normandy, when Cashel walked in, unannounced.

'Don't get on with locked doors, do you?' grinned Nat.

Cashel smiled as he sat down.

'Don't get on with a lot of things. People mainly.'

'So, what's up?'

'Not much. We still don't have anything to go on. When's your next trip?'

'Hard to say, but shouldn't be long, four or five days. Can't say I'm looking forward it.'

'You still okay with this? I mean…'

'Yeah, fine. Just talking about the travel. Anyway, I've got to take the artwork, and a model of the bottle, although actually I could Fed-Ex it, be a flipping hell of a lot…'

'No, no, no, trust a courier? Are you mad?' said Cashel sarcastically, 'You need to take it in person, so you do, safer.'

'Yeah, right.'

'Call me if anything happens, I'll be in touch.'

* * *

Nat resumed the call to Duvalle. He needed the production model as soon as possible.

Chapter Seven

'An investment in knowledge pays the best interest.'

Benjamin Franklin

It was a crisp, clear morning. Nat used his sleeve to sweep the dew from the seat and gunned the engine to life. It raced on full choke and threatened to wake his neighbours with its rhythmic, earthy rumble. He blasted his way along the deserted streets and headed north, out of the city and on to Normandy.

Ninety minutes later, flanked by open countryside, he whipped open the throttle and laughed aloud as the wind battered his unprotected face. He would soon arrive at his destination: Verreries Duvalle.

He slowed as he approached Gamaches and checked his mirror. The vintage BMW that had tailed him since L'Etoile was still there. He jumped the verge at the next bend, circled a barn and waited as the Beemer crept past and rolled to a halt a hundred yards up the road. White smoke billowed from the exhaust before it turned and headed slowly towards him. The rear wheel slipped as he dropped the clutch and raced to meet the car head on. He thought a collision was inevitable until the Beemer swerved at the very last second and dipped, nose first, down the narrow verge. Nat slammed the rear brake, spun the bike around and waited. The door swung open and a lanky figure hauled himself from the car.

* * *

'You stupid, fockin', eejit!' yelled Cashel, 'you could have fockin' killed me!'

Nat trundled towards him, grinning.

'You're getting slack, had you since L'Etoile...'

'I wasn't trying to hide, I was trying to fockin' catch you up!'

'Heh! That's funny! How come?'

'Can't talk here, there's a village up the…'

'Bouvaincourt.'

'Right, Bouvaincourt. Meet me there when you're done with the glass people.'

'Okay. They're not to be trusted, you know. The glass people.'

'What? Why? How can you tell?'

'I can see right through them.'

Cashel raised his arm to shield himself from the debris that flew from Nat's rear wheel. He shook his head and cursed. He was enjoying the company.

* * *

Emile was the latest in a long line of patriarchs who had run Duvalle since the 1860s. He greeted Nat with outstretched arms and a Gallic hug. They crossed the courtyard and paused by the old furnace room. A solitary figure toiled alone, blowing glass by hand. The stench of burning wood, sweat and Gauloises filled the air. Shafts of sunlight filtered through the timber roof and cut through the smoke. Nothing, it seemed, had changed in a hundred years. Nothing, apart from the newly erected timber and stone building across the way. The state-of-the-art factory was equipped with fully automated facilities for the manufacture of fragrance bottles. Emile ushered Nat inside. It was sterile and odourless. The only discernible sound was the delicate squeak of rubber on glass as mechanical squeegees branded bottles in a robotic frenzy. They crossed the floor to the meeting room where, atop the table, sat the final out-turns for 'Firebird'. The quality was superb and Emile reassured Nat that, with constant monitoring, they could keep the rejection rate to an acceptable level. Nat signed them off, thanked Emile with a vigorous handshake and headed for Bouvaincourt.

He killed the engine and coasted silently into the village. Cashel was seated outside the bar, sipping a '33'.

'Beer?'

'Sur la moto? Café,' said Nat.

'Sensible man. How'd it go?'

'Cool. Got the out-turns, all signed-off. So, come on then, what's up?'

'Kowolski. Remember Kowolski?'

'Yeah, the guy in New York.'

'Okay, so, we found a link with him and an outfit in Durban.'

'And…'

'What's South Africa famous for?'

'Apartheid? Diamonds? Gold? Ah, gold. Don't get it.'

'Let's say you have some gold, right? It's a worth a fortune but you'd rather have the cash. What do you do?'

'Sell it.'

'Right, but as soon as you try to sell it, the first question people ask is, "where did you get it?"'

'Ah,' said Nat. 'I see.'

'So you have to get rid of it with nobody knowing, kind of.'

'Got it. You think Kowolski is the behind the gold for 'Firebird'?'

'Not so fast, we don't know anything for sure, but we do have a hunch. If he is, then we're onto something very fockin' big.'

'And if he isn't?'

'Then it's very, very small.'

'Okay, so we're back to Rio then?'

'Soon as. Tomorrow?'

'If the artwork's done, sure, we could go tomorrow.'

'Grand! Okay, I'll sort the details out later. One more thing, before you go.' Cashel looked around while he fumbled in his jacket pocket, 'it's about time you had some protection, just in case.'

'In case…?'

'Things get out of hand. These aren't kids we're dealing with. Here, take this.'

Cashel pushed a jiffy bag across the table.

'You shouldn't have,' Nat quipped.

Frowning, he peeled apart the envelope and peeked inside. A shiny black pistol stared back.

'Ha-ha! Oh, no!' he said. 'No way! Forget it. Don't need it. All yours.'

'It's for your own safety. Trust me. You probably won't even use it.'

'I gave those up a long time ago, there is no way...'

Cashel leaned forward and stared intently at Nat.

'Take it. If it doesn't save you, it may save someone else,' he said sternly.

* * *

It was 6am. Terminal 2 was already crowded. With less than an hour before his flight, Nat went straight to the check-in desk. A severe-looking girl regarded him with a scowl as she took his passport and ticket. He wondered how the hell he'd get through security with a firearm strapped to his side. She glanced up as she lifted the phone and spoke softly.

'Moment, s'il vous plait,' she said. Within seconds, two men in plain suits appeared by his side. They said nothing. One took his grip, the other his passport and tickets. They led him through a side door and escorted him directly to the departure lounge. He was the last to board and, after a somewhat turbulent flight, the first to disembark.

Three stony-faced militia in peaked caps and chocolate-brown uniforms marched purposefully towards him as he approached immigration. They mumbled in Ukrainian as they flicked through his passport and handed him a succession of papers, demanding his signature on every one. He understood nothing, but recognised a likeness of himself on one sheet, next to Cashel's signature. Three minutes later, they handed him an official firearm permit and saluted him on his way.

* * *

It was early. Dinikin, hands clasped behind his back, was pacing the floor as Nat arrived. He appeared on edge. He stopped, faced Nat, and proffered his hand.

'Mr Pearson, so good to see you,' he said through tombstone teeth.

Behind him stood a man of older years. He wore a beard and smelled of beer and tobacco. The corner of his mouth twitched nervously and his hands were stained with printing ink. He was the rep from the firm that would produce the coffret for 'Firebird'. Dinikin clicked his fingers and beckoned him forward. It soon became clear that any business would be conducted without the comfort of a seat or the privacy of an office. Nat gave him a CD containing the artwork. He scurried away, vowing to return with a cromalin within the hour. He was barely out the door when Dinikin, too, made his excuses and left. Nat floundered. There was little to do but wait. He wandered the cobbled streets, stopped for a coffee, and wandered back. Dinikin was waiting, agitated, his mind elsewhere. He apologised for his demeanour and, by way of consolation, offered to show Nat round the factory before he left.

'After such a long journey, and all your hard work, it's only fair you see what we are doing here, Mr Pearson. After all, without you we would not have such a wonderful product.'

Fifteen minutes later, the rep returned. He passed Nat the cromalin.

'Well?' asked Dinikin. 'Is good, da?'

Feeling the pressure, Nat checked it over. He could find no fault.

'Yes,' he replied, 'it's good. I'm happy with that.'

'All systems go, Mr Pearson!' exclaimed Dinikin. 'Once again, I thank you. Now, if you'll excuse...'

Nat held his hand up and forced a smile.

'Thanks, I appreciate it, but what about the... you know, a look around?'

Dinikin raised his eyes skyward.

'Very well. Of course. I am forgetting. Come, we must be quick, I have much...'

His words tailed off as he hurried away. Nat raced to keep up with the diminutive Russian. Beyond the reception area they entered a large warehouse. Nat guessed three-thousand square feet, give or take. There were just four lines for sterilising, filling, sealing and packing the perfume bottles. For a limited edition, lead crystal decanter with, potentially, worldwide distribution, it appeared under-equipped. He let it go.

A large, roller shutter to the rear of the warehouse opened onto the loading bay. The area was a hive of activity. Nat steered Dinikin towards it so he could get a closer look. A fork-lift was unloading small, timber crates from a container and stacking them just two high in the bay. Each one was stencilled with wording he didn't understand, but recognised as Afrikaans.

Dinikin was rambling, his prior engagement forgotten.

'So, Mr Pearson, there you have it. If all goes well, we shall be launching in just a few days. Perhaps you should attend the launch as well. In fact, I insist.'

'Well, I... yes, yes, I'd be delighted.'

'Excellent. It will be a grand affair, lots of stars, like Hollywood!' he continued, hands cutting the air with enthusiasm. 'America. Land of opportunity. It will be my first visit, you know.'

'Really? That's... hold on, did you say America?'

'Of course! Where else? New York! So good they named it twice! I'll send you the details; now, I must go.'

Dinikin pointed towards a door.

'You'll find a way out through there.'

As he walked towards the exit, Nat heard the distinctive voice of someone from the Deep South. It was lilting, but loud and abrasive.

'C'mon Valery, where the hell you been, boy? We got work to do!'

Nat paused and glanced back. It was Kowolski, built like a wrestler with grey, crew-cut hair and a cauliflower ear. Beside him, hands in pockets, stood a younger man, mid-twenties, skinny but smart. They exchanged words as Dinikin approached, then disappeared from view.

* * *

Touchdown at 'de Gaulle came not a moment too soon. He spotted Cashel in the arrivals hall and followed him across the rain-lashed car park to his BMW. The rain drummed against the roof and bounced off the windscreen. He spoke, excitedly, of the previous day's events while Cashel stared into space, non-plussed.

'…and another thing, guess who was there? Guess? Kowolski! Kowolski! You were right, he looks a mean sonofa...'

'I know.'

'How do…'

'You're wearing a fockin' wire, remember?'

Nat paused.

'Oh yeah. Sorry. Okay, last thing, something you didn't hear. There was a shipment; from South Africa.'

'South Africa?'

'Yup. Wooden crates. Small. Heavy. Labelled in Afrikaans.'

'Gold.'

'Gold.'

Cashel rubbed his temple and tapped the steering wheel.

'How much?'

'A lot,' said Nat. 'Too much for the perfume, way too much.'

Cashel turned to Nat.

'And?' he asked.

'Guessing, but I reckon they were ingots; bars, not flake.'

'Okay. So, they got the gold to Kishinev. That was the easy part. Question is, how they gonna shift it? We're missing something here, Nat, we're missing something very fockin' obvious.'

'Maybe. Maybe not. Maybe we just have to wait.'

'Right enough, so you are. We'll wait. Look, you take off. I'll be in touch.'

* * *

Nat rose early. Sleep had not come easy. Something rankled him. He left for work, stopping en route, as usual, for a coffee at the bar. He aimed a quip about the litter on the street at the refuse collectors seated in the corner. The threat of a yard broom in his face alleviated his anxiety.

He spent the morning sifting through mail and staring down at the street below. He was contemplating lunch when the phone rang. An impromptu call from Verreries Duvalle. Emile wanted to know if Nat was aware of the changes in the specification for the Firebird decanters.

'Change? Non, Emile, qu'est-ce que c'est? What have they asked for?'

'It is Monsieur Dinikin, Nathan, he says the flacons will no longer be crystal.'

'Not crystal?'

'Oui, il veut quelque-chose leger, something light. Do we use tank glass?'

'Tank… well, yes, I suppose we could. Have you run any in the crystal yet?'

'Bien sûr! But not many; two hundred, perhaps.'

'Okay, look, Emile, put aside a few for me and run the rest in tank glass if that's what he wants. I'll try and reach him now, see what I can find out.'

'Très bien. Merci, Nathan. It's okay, isn't it? This job?'

'Sure, Emile, it's fine. Il y a pas lieu de s'inquièter. Okay?'

* * *

Nathan called Dinikin – no answer. He called again, and again, and again. After an hour he gave up. So far as he could see, there could only be two possible reasons for switching from crystal to tank glass: cost or timings. Either way, he concluded, he was not going to let it bother him further.

He walked down unfamiliar side streets, emptying his mind, when he came across a bar. It was scruffy and unkempt, bordering on dirty and hadn't had a lick of paint since the Liberation. The door creaked as he stepped inside. It stank of beer and stale tobacco. He rapped the bar with his knuckles and called for service. The sight of the proprietor knocked him for a six.

'What the f…!' yelled Nat.

'Bout ye?' grinned Cashel.

'What the hell are you… I mean…'

'Having trouble with your sentences?'

'I… I give up. What are you doing here? Moonlighting?'

'Very good. My place, so it is.'

'Your…? But you're a…'

'Barman. Nothing else. Remember that.'

Nat raised his eyebrows as the penny dropped.

'Say no more.'

Cashel grinned, opened two beers, passed one to Nat and raised his bottle.

'Salut,' he said. 'So, what brings you here, shouldn't you be drawing pictures or something?'

Nat smiled.

'Yeah, something like that; oh, fuck, actually I just got a call, this morning, from Duvalle, Dinikin's changed the spec'. They're not doing them in crystal anymore, just regular glass.'

'So, what does that mean?'

'God knows. Time? Cost, maybe?'

'Cost? Not with those fellas. They've got more fockin' money than the Vatican.'

Nat downed his beer.

'Gotta go,' he said, 'work to do.'

The door opened just as he stood to leave. A skinny man with a crooked nose and bandy legs strode across the floor like a cowpoke who'd lost a steer.

'Nat,' said Cashel, 'meet the hardest working bar-hand in the whole of Paris. Guillaume, meet Nat.'

* * *

An arrogant Frenchman was normal; a nervous one, out of character. Emile was unable to hide his anxiety.

Dinikin had ordered a second run, with the directive to ship the bottles to an address in New Jersey.

'Have you been paid?' asked Nat.

'Oui, hier,' said Emile.

'Then there's nothing to worry about. Tous va bien, Emile, tous va bien.'

For a second time, Nat dismissed the assumption that the extra order was down to increased sales and asked the more obvious question: why ship empty bottles to the States? It didn't make sense. The transmission that spewed from the fax urged Nat to Cashel's bar.

'They're launching day after tomorrow,' said Nat.

'Where?'

'Waldorf.'

Cashel pulled a crumpled sheet of A4 from his pocket and handed it to Nat.

'Take a look.'

Nat read the results of eight weeks' surveillance on Kowolski's activities. Three months earlier, he'd purchased, outright, an old bottling plant in New Jersey. By all accounts, it had been refurbed and upgraded but they couldn't say why. To confound them further, they were at a loss to explain the presence of armed security guards and a newly erected twelve-foot perimeter fence. Nat looked at Cashel.

'That address. That's where Duvalle has sent the bottles.'

'There's something else on its way too. Perfume, 'juice' as you call it.'

'How do you know?' asked Nat

'We know everything.'

'Sounds like they're gearing up to bottle it out there maybe, but why? It defeats the object of the exercise.'

Cashel looked at Nat and spoke quietly.

'There is no exercise. Never was.'

'So, what's next?'

'We're going on holiday.'

Chapter Eight

'I want to feel the sunlight on my face,
See that dust cloud disappear without a trace,
I want to take shelter from the poison rain,
Where the streets have no name.'

Bono (U2)

Nat took a final, lingering look around the apartment. The cigarettes were out, the appliances off and the ansafone on. He patted the Glock beneath his jacket and slammed the door behind him.

It was 5am. He banged the door to Cashel's bar. It swung open with ease. Cautiously, he peered inside. Bathed in the mellow light that filtered from the street stood Cashel, leaning on the bar, attired in a black suit.

'Jesus!' said Nat, 'what's this? You got a date?'

'You, my friend, don't recognise class when you see it. This… is Armani.'

'More like O'Marney, from where I'm standing.'

'Remind me to tell you about humour someday. You'll like it, so you will.'

Cashel stood to one side and summoned Nat to the bar. A neat row of papers lay before him. He passed them over, one by one.

'Return, Kennedy. Plane leaves in three and a half hours. It's open, in case you have to make your own arrangements… about coming back, that is.'

'Reassuring,' said Nat.

'Hotel, you'll be staying at the…'

'Royalton?'

'Howard Johnson. You'll not know the difference.'

'And the envelope?'

'Cash. Six thousand dollars. You might need to buy your way out, but it's not a shopping trip, okay? Keep the fockin' receipts.'

Cashel reached in his pocket, produced a small piece of paper and handed it to Nat.

'Finally, and most importantly, phone number. Memorise it, destroy it and don't fockin' use it unless you really have to,' he waved it under Nat's nose, 'call this and you'll have everyone from the CIA to the National Guard on your arse. Understand?'

'Da! Anything else?'

'Outside. Across the street, there's a black Peugeot. He'll take you to the airport. Have a good trip.'

* * *

The clerk at the Air France check-in desk was overshadowed by a rotund fifty-something who instantly seized Nat's passport and ticket. 'Venez avec moi, Monsieur Pearson. Venez! Vite! Vite!'

He was led the length of the check-in desks and through a door marked 'Personnes Autorisées' to the confines of a small office. An officer of the Gendarmerie Nationale sat alone at a desk. He addressed Nat without looking up.

'Your weapon, please, Mr Pearson. You cannot travel with a firearm in the cabin. It will be returned to you when you reach New York.'

Nat surrendered the gun, the clip was discharged and the rounds counted out and logged. The spare rounds followed suit. They were neatly placed in a black, metal box which was sealed and marked with the stamp of officialdom.

He noticed a familiar face as he boarded the flight. Familiar, but he couldn't place him. Until an hour later. Kishinev. The loading bay. It was the fellow he'd seen with Kowolski.

* * *

Kennedy International. The plane hit the deck like a legless goose. Nat was escorted to a trailer, airside, where Cashel and his men were waiting. Two of New York's Finest, each carrying a black, metal box, joined them seconds later and the firearms were systematically returned to their rightful owners. A short, stocky man dressed in a worn, leather bomber, faded jeans and sneakers, clambered into the already cramped trailer and blocked their exit.

'Okay guys, listen up and listen good!'

He rubbed his ample belly and continued.

'First off, welcome to New York City. My name is Angelini. Think of me as your angel and you won't forget the name. I am DEA. We are on the same side.

Furthermore, we are all after the same guys, so, let's play ball, eh?'

Cashel stood, zipped his jacket and looked at Angelini.

'My name's Cashel. We are Interpol. Look at my face, you'll not see it again.'

* * *

He ushered his men towards the door. Angelini smiled through tight lips as they filed by. Cashel stopped and whispered in his ear.

'This is bigger than drugs, Angel. Don't fock it up for us.'

They huddled by the trailer as Cashel delivered a simple briefing.

'Right,' he said, 'it's now, exactly, nine-o-three. Go to your hotels, check-in, get some rest and wait for the call. Do not go out. Do not go to Molly's. And do not go to Bloomingdales. You're all big enough to look after yourselves, so, away with you.'

The group dispersed, Cashel to the Avis desk and Nat to the taxi rank. The cab spat him out directly in front of the Howard Johnson on Allen Street. A black dude, from 1972, accosted him on the sidewalk.

'Hey, looky here, check it out, fly-guy, wan' some shit? Wan' some coke to smoke?'

His suit was white, his teeth gold. Nat smiled, drew on his cigarette and glanced up the street. It took just as long for the peddler to disappear.

Nat checked in. The concierge gave him a message. It wasn't from Cashel, and he was the only one who knew he was staying at the HoJo. He waited in the lobby, waited for Cashel to call. Half an hour later, a figure slinked through the main door and crossed the lobby to the elevator. Nat recognised him instantly. It was the guy he'd seen on the plane. The guy with Kowolski in the loading bay. Nat moved swiftly and collared him from behind.

'Make a sound and the next thing you hear will your neck snapping,' he whispered through gritted teeth.

'Get the fuck off me man, you wanna…?'

Nat tightened his grip.

'Who are you? What's your name?' growled Nat.

'Okay, okay. Granger. It's Granger!' he choked.

Nat released him, rammed his face against the flocked wallpaper and held him in a thumb-lock. Granger winced as his digit reached breaking point.

'I'm one of you, please, I'm with Cashel.'

It didn't make sense. He couldn't be. Nat whispered in his ear, close enough to bite it off.

'Let's go. Take me to him. Now.'

* * *

The hotel was a five-minute walk away, around the corner, on The Bowery. A fizzling neon sign above the entrance blinked erratically. The front door opened directly onto a staircase.

'He's in twenty-eight,' said Granger. 'Honest. Twenty-eight.'

Nat glanced up the stairs.

'Get lost,' he said.

Nat went up to the first floor. It was a glorified doss house. No reception, just a couple of flea-bitten sofas and a soda machine. A fat man in a vest with a face like Play-Doh, sat behind a hatch. Nat breezed by and headed for room twenty-eight. He took a deep breath and burst in. Cashel was seated on the edge of the bed.

'What the fock are you doing here?!' he hissed, leaping from the bed and slamming the door.

'News. Big news. We need to talk.'

'How did you find me?'

'That's another story. Got any coffee?'

'Coffee? Are you joking me? What's up?'

'They know we're here,' said Nat.

'What? Talk sense you fockin' eejit, who knows we're here?'

'There was a message, waiting for me, at the hotel. That means they knew I was coming. They knew where I'd be staying.'

'Who?'

'Susie Hernandez.'

'What? Hernan... How the fock does she... What does she want?'

'Didn't say, just left a number. It's a 212. She's right here, in Manhattan.'

Cashel sat back down and rubbed his chin.

'Hold on, just a minute here. What if she called your office, could they have told her where...'

'No chance. They have no idea where I am.'

'Then… then she's here for the launch, but that doesn't explain how she knew where to reach you...'

'Exactly. Unless someone told her, someone that did know.'

'Someone that did... fock! What're you saying? Are you saying what I think you're saying?'

'What I'm saying is, there may be someone on the inside.'

'Cheer me up, why don't you. No ideas I suppose?'

Nat paused before answering.

'Granger.'

'Granger? Nah, he's one of…'

'One of them, maybe. He was in Kishinev.'

'I know, he was meant to be in Kishinev.'

'With Kowolski.'

'Oh.'

* * *

The radio in Cashel's jacket crackled to life. He acknowledged the call and switched it off.

'Let's go,' he said to Nat. 'Angel face. He's got news from Paris.'

Angelini was waiting as they arrived at Police Plaza. He led them through a maze of corridors to a vast office on the third floor.

'You guys want something? Coffee, donut maybe?' he asked.

Cashel shook his head.

'Suit yourself. Here, take a look at this, probably means more to you than it does to me.'

They gathered round a Mac.

'We just got this surveillance through, from Paris, France. I recognise him, Kowolski, that's easy. I am thinking, maybe, you could help us with the others.'

The first three shots showed Kowolski, clear as daylight at Zurich International Airport. He was with a woman, a small woman.

'The dame,' said Angelini, 'any idea who she is?'

'Her name's Hernandez. Suzie Hernandez,' said Cashel. 'Run a check on her, she's here. In Manhattan. See if you can get an address.'

'That's very helpful, thank you,' said Angelini. 'Okay, just one more. It ain't great, they said they had to "enhance the image", so it only just came through now. Anyone you know? Can you help with these?'

It was the Boulevard Hausmann. Night time. Two figures stood by a streetlamp, shaking hands. Smiling. One was Dinikin. The other, Granger.

'Sorry,' said Cashel, 'can't help you, there.'

* * *

They left the building. Cashel spoke as they walked hastily uptown.

'Okay,' he said, 'listen. You and me, we're going to Jersey, take a look at that plant. Not a word to anyone, understand?'

They stopped at a hot-dog vendor.

'Course,' said Nat. 'Hot-dog? Gyro?'

'What the fock is a Gyro?'

* * *

It was dusk. The city sparkled as the streetlamps burst to life. They rumbled through the traffic, high up in the Explorer. By the time they exited the Holland Tunnel, it was night. Route 78 led them to Irvington, a forgotten town with boarded-up stores and empty streets. They slowed to a crawl. A lone figure, clutching a brown paper bag, zig-zagged his way along the sidewalk. Nat tapped the dash and pointed ahead. Floodlights bathed the plant in a ferocious, foreboding light. They slumped in their seats and cruised by the perimeter fence. It was twelve feet high, steel, with a razor wire finish. Security guards ambled back and forth, radios clipped to their chests, Kalashnikovs slung across their shoulders. Cashel drove by, killed the lights and pulled up.

'We need a way in,' he said.

They sat in silence and waited. Forty minutes later a UPS truck trundled by. It stopped just short of the main gates.

'Let's go! Come on, quick!' whispered Cashel. 'Stay low.'

They crouched by the kerb.

'Walk up, like you've had a skinful. Pee on his wheel. Say nothing.'

Nat sauntered to the front of the truck, smiled at the driver and pretended to unzip his fly.

'Hey, buddy, hey! What the fuck are you… stop that, you sonofa…!'

The driver leapt from his seat, slid open the door and jumped to the sidewalk. Nat took a step back and raised his hands. Cashel delivered a single, sharp blow to the back his head and caught him as he collapsed. Dressed in his jacket and cap, he took to the wheel and signalled Nat to stay back.

Cashel waved a clipboard at the sentry on the gate who duly raised the barrier and waved them in. He parked by the loading bay, grabbed a parcel and went in search of a signature. Nat followed at a discreet distance, undetected, and met Cashel inside. Cautiously, they ventured deeper into the plant. Loud voices struggled to be heard over the sound of crashing glass. They peered, tentatively, over a stack of crates. A workforce of six or seven Moldavian-looking men were throwing bottles into a large, rotating steel drum. A forklift almost revealed their whereabouts as it hoisted two crates from the stack. Nat stabbed Cashel with his elbow and nodded towards the drum. The bottles were 'Firebird' flacons. They regarded each other with a look of utter confusion. Cashel sank to the floor and shrugged his shoulders. Nat frantically prised open one the crates and liberated a flacon. His jaw dropped in a state of elation. He passed the bottle for Cashel to inspect. There was no juice, no perfume. Just a beautifully shaped, solid gold ingot.

'Tank glass!' hissed Nat.

'What?'

'Tank... don't you see? It's tank glass! Look, they changed the spec', right? From lead crystal to tank glass? For Chrissakes! It's the weight! The difference in weight, between lead crystal and tank glass, is like a feather and a pound of potatoes! Shit, that's smart, oh boy, I'm telling ya, that's fuckin' smart.'

'So, you're saying they're importing gold?' said Cashel.

'They're smuggling the fucking gold! Don't you...'

'They're... Jesus, got you! The gold compensates for the difference in weight. It tallies on the paperwork and they're home free! Genius.'

'At last!'

'You clever wee... how much d'you think there is here?'

'How the fuck should I know?'

'Okay, okay, just thinking out loud. Come on, let's get a closer look.'

* * *

A gantry, six feet from the roof, ran the periphery of the building, offering them the perfect vantage point. They scaled the staircase and crawled on their bellies to get a view of the action from thirty feet up. They watched as the drum ground the glass, leaving the gold to be retrieved and despatched for, they assumed, smelting elsewhere. Nat grinned in twisted admiration as he spotted yet more shipments of, this time, empty bottles, being filled with essence, packaged and boxed, ready for shipping.

They'd seen enough. Cashel nodded towards a fire door at the end of gantry. From the parapet on the roof, they watched the security guards below scatter like ants, shouting and swearing. The driver of the UPS van was frog-marched across the yard. It was time to go. Their only feasible exit was a vertical descent, courtesy of a fire-ladder that ran all the way to the ground. Nat enthusiastically climbed over the edge first. 'Like this,' he said as he pulled his cuffs over his hands, placed his feet on the outside edge of the rungs and slackened his grip. He slid to the ground at breakneck speed and hit the deck in a heartbeat. Cashel followed at a more sedate pace, choosing instead to descend one step at a time, until a hail of bullets peppered the wall above his head. He barely touched the ladder as he crashed to the ground and instinctively pulled his weapon from the sanctuary of his armpit.

He joined Nat in a counter assault. They held their ground and, with single shots, picked off their targets, one by one. Six assailants lay in their wake as they scaled the boundary fence and ran to the car. The smell of burning rubber hung heavy in the air as they screeched their way into the night.

'What a craic!' screamed Cashel. 'Better than the fockin' pub, eh?'

'Okay, calm down! What now?'

'I don't know. Will we steal a car maybe, rob a liquor store…?'

'Or go home. I'm beat, what say we call it a night?'

'Call it a... and I thought you knew how to party.'

Three blocks later they slowed to a respectable speed and passed a posse of squad cars screaming in the opposite direction. No doubt someone had complained about the noise.

* * *

The following morning, Cashel was rudely awakened by an over-inquisitive Angelini, demanding to know if he'd been involved with the previous night's events. Despite his disdain for the abrasive American, Cashel realised he needed his help and co-operated as best he could. They arranged to meet as a matter of urgency. Nat joined them at the hotel. Between them, they devised a plan of action.

Strike One: The bottling plant in Jersey. Hit it hard, create maximum confusion with scatter-fire, flares and noise. Impound the contraband and detain every single individual on the premises.

Strike Two: Firebird launch. Waldorf Astoria. Attend the party. Wait for confirmation that the bottling plant had been secured. Secrete away Dinikin and Kowolski.

Strike Three: They're out.

* * *

Nat was the natural choice as the man on the inside. Dinikin had already made it clear that he was to be an integral part of the launch. He knew the high-rolling, chowder-heads who would be in attendance would love nothing more than to waste money on a product from a country they'd never heard of, designed by someone they'd never met, at a price that ensured it remained the domain of the privileged few.

Nat was under orders to keep both him and Kowolski occupied, thus preventing them from hearing about the bust at the plant. The whole team would be wired. 'If all else fails,' said Cashel, 'just make it up as you go along.'

An hour before dusk, Cashel and his team met with Angelini and his in the parking lot beneath Police Headquarters. The cold, concrete surroundings and economical use of light lent a sinister air to the proceedings. They huddled round the hood of a Dodge, listened to Angelini's brief, and made mental notes of where they should be, and when. The teams eyed each other with a degree of scepticism and extreme competitiveness. Angelini's crew were dressed for combat in body armour and baseball caps, headsets and shiny boots. Each had a square jaw, a crotch-full of testosterone and enough weaponry to take out a small country. Cashel's gang of four resembled a group of lawless terrorists, dressed to kill in black, knitted, skull-caps pulled down to their eyebrows. They wore no armour, their weapons concealed beneath their coats. Angelini felt intimidated. He had a hunch they could probably take out his entire team with a single shot from their nine millimetres.

Briefing over, Cashel split his team into two. One group of three, and Granger with him. They left in two trucks. One in the colours of Con-Edison, the other, an unmarked Dodge.

Nat arrived at the Waldorf. Ahead of him lay an evening devoid of alcohol, just when he needed Uncle Jack most. He made his way to the Grand Ballroom where an out-of-work actor relieved him of his invitation. He maintained a low profile and hovered by the door, sipping spring water. Dinikin spotted him from a private box on the balcony. A gaggle of sycophants trailed in his wake as he raced down towards him, intoxicated.

'Mr Pearson!' he shouted, 'Nathan, my dear friend, you've arrived!'

Embarrassed by the attention foisted upon him, Nat bowed his head and took a deep breath. Dinikin was out to impress, out to impress anyone foolish enough, and young enough, to be taken in.

'Dinikin. How's things?'

'Things are, how do you say, hunky dory! I love this country! I love America! Come, I have people dying to meet you!'

Dinikin introduced Nat to his new-found friends, friends who will have forgotten his name by morning. The CEOs and creatives, the account handlers and the ad men, the journalists and the photographers. Nat smiled politely, abstained from conversation and avoided eye-contact with the silicon-enhanced twenty-somethings that flanked Dinikin. His mind was elsewhere, on the other side of The Hudson.

* * *

The Con-Edison truck coasted silently to a halt and parked within spitting distance of Cashel's UPS hijack, twenty-fours earlier. It was, perhaps, tempting fate, but there was no better place to be should circumstance dictate a hasty retreat. The unmarked Dodge cruised by and stopped a hundred yards farther down the street. Both teams slipped silently from the trucks and embraced the darkness. They slinked like sewer rats into the compound and took up their positions.

Cashel led Granger up the ladder to the roof where they could 'monitor events and provide cover for those on the ground'. He knew, regrettably, that tonight he would have to terminate his employment. They knelt behind the parapet and waited for the fireworks to begin. Five minutes passed. Ten. Fifteen. Granger was sweating.

'I think I should go down,' he said. 'We don't have enough men on the ground.'

'Scared of heights?' said Cashel, without looking up.

'No, I just think, if…'

'Don't think. It's bad for your health, so it is.'

'Look, I really…'

Cashel turned and glared at him with icy eyes.

'Call Kowolski,' he said, 'ask him for back-up.'

Granger turned white, a wave of unadulterated fear washed over his body. He knew that in order to remain breathing he had to escape. He made a desperate lunge at Cashel, hoping to knock him off balance and then from the roof. His actions were clumsy and ill-judged. Cashel grabbed him by the collar and pulled him onto his back. He stood and placed a foot across his throat. Granger smiled. Cashel swiftly raised his boot and brought it down with all the force he could muster. There was a crack as it smashed Granger's nose and shattered his cheekbone. Below him, the sound of gunfire rattled across the yard. He leaned out over the roof to survey the situation. Behind him came the subtle click of a safety catch being released. In a single movement, he whipped the Glock from his holster, turned and fired. A nine-millimetre hole appeared in Granger's head.

He dropped to the ground where more bodies littered the yard than could ever be deemed fair. The wail of sirens grew louder as a fleet of squad cars screamed down the street. Cashel got his team into the van while Angelini directed the cops around the site. Before long, the plant was secure.

The two trucks sped towards the Holland Tunnel and the bright lights of Manhattan. Strike One was complete.

Chapter Nine

'A castle, called Doubting Castle,
the owner, whereof, was Giant Despair.'

Bunyan

Kowolski spurned the launch. His was not a face to be recognised. Instead, he remained firmly ensconced in a Tower Suite on the thirty-second floor. He chuckled as he contemplated the profit from the gold and lit a Cohiba. The phone rang. His face turned a purple shade of rage as an anonymous voice relayed the events at the bottling plant. His mind became addled as it juggled the consequences. He paced the room, punching the air like a boxer landing body blows, before returning to the desk and stuffing his passport and wallet into his pockets. He called his CPA and ordered the transfer of all his funds to an account in Geneva. Finally, he summoned Dinikin on the house phone.

'Valery! You listen up, boy! We about to have us some company and they ain't invited, you understand what I'm sayin'? Good! Now, don't you go doin' nothing rash, you treat 'em real nice, ya hear? I mean, real nice, and you bring 'em right here to me. Got it? Right here.'

Dinikin knocked back his vodka, too drunk to realise the severity of the words.

* * *

The tyres screeched as the van cornered the down-ramp and slewed to halt in the parking lot beneath the hotel. Cashel jumped from the cab, taped a wire to his midriff and donned a lounge suit. Angelini's van pulled up alongside.

'Wait for the word, okay?' said Cashel.

Angelini nodded.

Cashel breezed into the ballroom and smiled politely as he weaved his way through the crowd and took up a position by the fire exit. He spotted Nat just as the lights dimmed and Dinikin stumbled onto the stage. His speech was slurred, his ramblings, unintelligible, his moment of glory cut short as a three-litre 'Firebird' flacon was lowered from the ceiling accompanied by a deafening fanfare. The crowd whooped and applauded through dry ice and flashing lights.

* * *

Nat declined the offer of lunch with Donna Karan and an invitation to work with Calvin Klein. He knew the fragrance wouldn't hit the streets. He knew that this would be it. The diminutive Dinikin danced his way towards him.

'They love it, Pearson! They love you!'

'Take it easy, comrade,' said Nat, 'the world'll be a colder place in the morning, believe me.'

'Whatever. You think I can claim political asylum?'

'Who knows?'

'No matter, come with me! There is someone I want you to meet, the person who made this whole thing possible...'

'But I thought, Hernandez...'

'Forget Hernandez, like I said, he got greedy. Come. Come, come.'

He led Nat by the arm to the elevator. They got off at the thirty-second floor. Dinikin, swaying on his feet, rapped the door and waited for a reply. Kowolski had company. Two men with shaven heads in black suits stood with their backs to the wall. Their tight-fitting jackets outlined the holsters beneath their arms. Nat made a mental note of their accessories and adopted a stance by the door.

'What in the name of sweet Jesus are you doin' here?' yelled Kowolski. 'I told you we was expecting company! Now git! If...'

Dinikin raised his hands in defence.

'Yes, yes, I know, but this is Mr Pearson, the designer! Without him, we… you owe it to him... they loved us, Kowolski, you should have seen...'

'Okay, okay. You, fella, nice to meet ya son, make your acquaintance and all, but I'm kinda busy right now. I'm expecting company.'

'No problem. Sorry, I missed your name…'

'Name? Don't matter who I am, boy! Ah, what the heck, here, shake. Kowolski's the name. I'm the damn fool behind this whole nancy scheme.'

Nat stepped forward, shook Kowolski's paddle-sized hand, and stepped back.

'You? Sorry, I thought Hernandez was the brains behind...' said Nat.

'Not no more, he ain't... say, you ever meet that crazy sonofabitch?'

'Hernandez? Yeah, coupla times.'

'Hmm. Don't suppose he mentioned his ol' buddy Kowolski, did he?'

'Nope, can't say he did.'

'Sonofa... don't matter none. Now look, son, like I say, I got company.'

* * *

The door crashed open. Cashel and Angelini strode in. They stood, three feet apart, eyeing everyone in the room. Kowolski, relaxed, leant back in his chair.

'Well, looky here, come on in, boys, I've been expecting you! Kinda on your lonesome, ain't ya? Valery, take this fella back to the party, give the boy a drink. I got business to attend to.'

Dinikin took Nat by the arm and steered him towards the door. Cashel acknowledged the monkeys by the wall.

'Nice suit there, fellas. Goes with the hair.'

'Trying to be funny, boy?' said Kowolski. 'Don't sound too funny to me.'

He stood, anger welling up inside him.

'Do you know how much grief you caused me? Are you aware of the inconvenience I have suffered because of you? Hell, no, didn't think you did. Now, here's the thing, I understand you's a lawman and all but that don't mean nothing to me. Where I come from, I am the law.'

He looked at Nat and scowled.

'You, designer-boy, I ain't gonna ask again. Now git.'

Nat turned to go, paused, and turned round again.

'Actually,' he said quietly, 'I think I'll stay.'

'What! Are you some kinda crazy fool? I told you to... oh hey! Hold on there, just a minute, you ain't mixed up in this thing too, are ya?'

'Huh?'

'You is! My, my, you is a fool. Well now, you's a dead fool.'

Kowolski glanced at his henchmen and nodded.

'Boys. Take 'em out.'

By the time they'd taken a single step, it was already too late. Angelini stood, bewildered, as Nat and Cashel unleashed a volley of fire. The henchmen jerked and flailed like busted marionettes, before they fell, dead. Kowolski seized his chance, knocked Angelini to the floor and bounded down the corridor with surprising speed. Nat spun to face the desk as a whimpering Dinikin emerged on all fours.

'Stay down! Lie flat! Arms out!' he yelled. 'What's up with Angel? He dead?'

'Nah,' said Cashel, 'sore head, is all. Hey! Angel! Get the fock up!'

Angelini stood, surveyed the bodies and scratched the back of his head.

'You know how much paperwork this is gonna take?' he said.

* * *

Angelini frog-marched Dinikin to his truck and sped back to Police Plaza. Cashel and Nat went in search of Kowolski. Having scoured the ballroom, and then the streets, they knew, deep down, their search was futile. Kowolski was long gone.

Cashel called Angelini to request an APB and a block on all ports. The response wasn't what he'd expected.

'Ain't necessary! Get your ass down here, I got a better idea!' he said.

Angelini was sitting at his desk, feet up, smoking a cheroot. He grinned as they walked in.

'What is it?' asked Cashel. 'You find Kowolski?'

'Did I find Kowolski? No, not yet.'

'Where's Dinikin?'

'Where's Dinikin? That's very good. Where's Dinikin? I let him go!'

'You... you let him what? Are you fockin'...'

'Hey, hey, hey, listen up, hear me out, okay?'

Cashel sat down. His eyes narrowed as he stared at Angelini.

'Go on,' he said.

'It's easy. Look, Dinikin, he's scared, right? I mean, he's so scared, the maggot wanted asylum, already. He pleaded ignorance, says he's just a... just an employee. A gofer. So I says: Dinikin, if you are telling me the truth, if you are just a gofer, then you mean nothing to me. You are free to go. Get the fuck outta here!'

'Oh, that's smart, so it is. Very fockin' smart.'

'Thank you. That's how we do things round here. We use our heads. Right now, we are tailing him. Why? Because he will lead us straight to Kowolski.'

Cashel spoke quietly, through gritted teeth.

'Now, here's the thing, Angel. See, you've made the wrong assumption, there. Dinikin is small-fry. The reason he's scared, is cos Kowolski don't give a shit about him. Cos he knows enough to put Kowolski away. Cos he knows Kowolski is after him. He doesn't have a fockin' clue where Kowolski is!'

'Really? I never looked at it like...'

'We have to protect him so we can convict him, you fockin' eejit!'

'Okay, enough! We got a tail on him. I'll tell them to bring him in.'

'Do it now!'

Angelini made a call. They patched him through to the tail. He hung up.

'They, er, they lost him,' he said.

'What?' hissed Cashel. 'How? How could that happen?'

'I don't know, I...'

Cashel stood up, ruffled his hair and rubbed his chin. He leant on the desk, his face inches from Angelini's.

'A waste,' he whispered. 'This whole fockin' trip, a complete waste. And it's all thanks to you.'

He turned to go.

'C'mon, Nat, we're away. There's nothing more we can do here. Angel, listen to me now, we are going back to our hotels, packing our bags and heading home. If you hear anything, anything at all, you get in touch, understand?'

* * *

Exhausted, they slept for most of the flight aboard an Air France 747, unaware of the news they'd left behind. The first edition of *The New York Post* was hitting the stands. Tucked away on page nine, was a story over which no-one would weep.

'Russian Shot: Cops were called to an incident at Seventy-Second and Columbus shortly after 1am. The body of a Soviet national, identified as Mr Valery Dinikin, was found face down, outside the Pioneer store. A single shot to the back of the head caused the fatal wound. Police are appealing for witnesses.'

* * *

Nat cautiously pushed the door aside and peered down the hall. Like most people returning from a trip, he half expected to see something new, something different, something awry. There were no surprises, the apartment was just as he'd left it. He dropped his grip in the hallway, threw open the windows and showered briskly. The Marlboro fizzled as he slumped on the couch and, eventually, fell asleep.

It was after eleven when he woke; the moon was high and the sky was clear. A chill ran through the apartment. He closed the windows, dressed headed off through the deserted streets of Montparnasse.

'Bout ye?' said Cashel. The bar was empty.

'Fine,' said Nat. 'You?'

'Been better, so I have, but I'll get over it.'

They grinned and shook hands. Cashel poured two Bushmills.

'Slàinte!' he said.

'Cheers!' Nat downed it in one. 'So, what happens now?'

'What happens now? Nathan, my friend, you've a way with words, so you have, and the answer is: I don't fockin' know!'

'Honesty. I like that, Poirot, I like it.'

'Truth is, I reckon the whole thing's banjaxed. You know Dinikin's dead, don't you?'

'No? When?'

'Yesterday. Bullet, back of the head.'

'Hit?'

'Has to be.'

'Kowolski?'

'No-one else in the frame.'

'Shame. I kind of liked him, in a way. He was harmless.'

Cashel raised his eyebrows and refilled the glasses.

'You're getting soft.'

Nat grinned.

'I'm getting old. So, that's it then? All over?'

'Maybe. Maybe not. We lie low and wait.'

'How long?'

'Long as it takes. Meantime, go back to being a civilian.'

Chapter Ten

'Out of the strong,
came forth sweetness.'

Book of Judges

The warmth of the vestry left Nat cold. He didn't trust in God. He didn't trust the church. The Chesterfield creaked as he tried to concentrate on Cashel's words, the sound of the dead 'priest's' head hitting the pew still echoed in his ears.

'Your man, out front, he wasn't picked by God, you know that, right?'

'Yeah, figured that. You know him?'

'Never seen him before.'

'Then he's working for Kowolski, right?'

'Not necessarily.'

'Well, who else then? There's no-one else who could possi—'

Cashel raised his hand and took a deep breath.

'Hernandez.'

Nat's face creased in surprise.

'What?' he hissed. 'He's fucking dead! What do you…?'

'Catch yourself. He faked it.'

'No shit.'

'No shit.'

'Holy shit. Why?'

'Kowolski. Hernandez had him on the payroll, Kowolski got greedy, wanted the whole deal for himself, so, figured he'd get rid of him.'

'And Hernandez got out before Kowolski got the chance?'

'In one. Thing is, Hernandez see, he doesn't exactly hold Kowolski responsible for the deal going tits up. He's after us.'

'Us? You are kidding me? How come?'

'If we hadn't interfered, he'd be a couple of mil' better off by now.'

'Un-believable. Fucking sore loser or what? So, he's too scared to go after Kowolski?'

'That's about the size of it.'

'And he wants to take us out? That's his revenge?'

'There is an upside. It means we may have a chance to nail Hernandez after all.'

They eyed each other earnestly. Each knew there was no way out, each knew neither was leaving, and each knew they had to finish the job. The atmosphere was strained. Cashel broke the silence.

'Nat, I'd like to walk away from this as much as you, but what's the point of running if you're on the wrong road?'

'True. You've got to go, to come,' said Nat.

'We think Hernandez is here. Marseille, possibly.'

Nat gazed down at his boots and scratched the tip of his nose.

'So, he's in Marseille. His gorillas are here. What's next?'

'We're disappearing. You and me. A long spell away, somewhere incognito. As soon as they get Hernandez, we can get our lives back.'

'So we can go? Now?'

'Aye. The hotel. There'll be a ride for us soon enough.'

'I need a drink.'

'You and me both. C'mon. Nice and easy though. Nice and easy.'

* * *

Cashel stood, unzipped his cassock and let it drop to the floor. He was dressed, head to toe, in black. An ammunition belt and two side-arms hung from his waist.

'You putting on weight?' asked Nat.

'It's the uniform. Kill the lights.'

Cashel gently turned the handle and opened the door less than half an inch. In less time than was humanly possible to calculate, a succession of bullets splintered the architrave above his head. Just as quickly, Nat kicked his legs out from under him and brought him crashing to the floor. They slammed the door shut and shuffled back into the vestry.

'How many?' asked Nat.

'Three. Maybe four.'

Their eyes slowly became accustomed to the darkness as they sat and waited. Ten minutes passed, then fifteen, twenty, twenty-five, thirty. The silence was oppressive.

'I can't take much more of this,' whispered Nat, 'why don't they just...'

A hail of bullets pierced the door and ricocheted off the plaster walls. Glass and splinters showered the floor. They crouched, stock still, barely breathing. The door inched open. A large figure in a balaclava took a tentative step inside. A second, smaller figure followed close behind. He fumbled, carelessly, for the light switch. A flash of light filled the room for a millisecond before Cashel shot out the bulb and Nat took care of their would-be assassins. They dropped to the floor, each two bullets heavier.

'Leave one for me, next time,' croaked Cashel, 'you don't have to do it all yourself!'

'Shhh!'

'Ah, shhh yourself! I don't fockin' need this. I need the fockin' toilet.'

'Cheeks together, you'll be fine. Look. There's one, maybe two more, right?'

'Right. Any less just wouldn't be fair now, would it?'

'So, we have a choice.'

'We do?'

'We sit tight, or we can go. If we wait, there's every chance we'll still be here at dawn. If that's the case, then everything's cool. They won't hang around when it gets light.'

'True enough, but you're forgetting, the lads'll be here soon.'

'I ain't forgetting. Thing is, if we ain't at the hotel, they ain't gonna hang around. Which brings me to our other option.'

'Jesus, Mary and Joseph. I can see where this is going.'

'So, we go. Make a break for it. All we have to do is make it to the front door. Down the aisle, and out the door.'

They stood, either side of the door, backs to the wall, pistols pointing towards the ground. Cashel glanced at Nat with reassuring grin.

'See you outside then,' he said.

'Better had,' replied Nat, 'better had.'

He mimed a countdown. On 'three', Nat bolted for his life, Cashel on his tail. They raced down the aisle as someone opened fire from above. Tiles shattered as shells sprayed the floor beneath them. The first bullet hit Cashel in the back. He swore under his breath as a second tore into his thigh, sending him spinning to the ground. A third struck him in the chest before he hit the floor. Nat spontaneously dropped to his knees and let loose an entire clip in the direction of the assailant. He scrambled towards Cashel who lay, motionless, on his back.

'I can't be certain,' he said, 'but I think I may have been hit.' His chin, daubed with crimson, glistened in the dim light. 'Get the fock out, I'll be fine.'

'Like hell,' said Nat 'you're coming with me.'

He hauled Cashel over his shoulder and struggled valiantly towards the security of the street. With twenty yards to go, two, single, precisely-aimed shots struck Cashel in the back. The impact sent them both crashing to the floor. The church fell silent. Cashel looked up at Nat.

'Now, will you listen, you fockin' arse?' he said.

With that, his head lolled to one side and his eyes glazed over.

The air turned blue as Nat swore and screamed, emptying another clip as he sprinted for the door. Across the square, in front of the hotel, was Cashel's BMW, engine running. He ran towards the open door and jumped in.

'Où est Cashel!' screamed the driver as he floored the gas and took refuge in the darkness of the countryside. 'Où est Cashel!' he asked again.

Confused, angry and in shock, Nat wiped his face with his hands. He answered slowly as he raised his eyes to the driver.

'He's, I think he's... Holy Crap! What the fuck are you doing here?'

'Please, Nathan, my friend, please try to relax...'

'Relax! How can I fuckin' relax when... you! Jesus! Anyone else I know mixed up in this shit?'

'No, no, I don't think so,' said Guillaume, 'just me. I hope.'

Guillaume slowed to sensible speed and spoke quietly.

'Nathan, you must listen to me. Are you listening? Good, we do not have much time; you are in great danger, you must leave immediately.'

'Are you crazy? What about Lennie? And Jack? I've got to…'

'Ecoutez Nathan! The department will finish this, d'accord? Right now, we must go to the airport.'

'Airport? No way, I have to see Jack…'

'She is waiting for you.'

'What? Why is she…? Don't get her involved in this!'

'We haven't. Unfortunately, Monsieur Hernandez, he has.'

'Hernandez? What the fuck's going on, Guillaume?'

'He's having her watched. It's okay, we are watching them. It is possible Hernandez may try to get to you through her.'

'Crap! Fucking crap! How much have you told her? How much does she know?'

'She will know only what you choose to tell her. We have said nothing.'

'She's at the airport?'

'Mais oui. You are both going to have a nice long vacance.'

Nat sat back and closed his eyes. A couple of minutes passed.

'Okay. Okay,' he said calmly, 'where we headed?'

'Beauvais, mon ami, Beauvais.'

'I don't mean the airport, for Chrissakes, I mean...'

'I know exactly what you mean. You should know better than to ask a question like that.'

* * *

The blue flashing lights danced and bounced across the sodden tarmac as they raced towards the plane. Standing on the apron was a 757 in Air France livery. Three gendarmes stood guard on the stairway. Guillaume slew the car to a halt at the foot of steps. He turned to Nat.

'This is it, Nathan. Everything you need is on board, we even packed a bag for you! One last thing, you are not to worry, we will not rest until this is over, d'accord?'

'Sure. Adieu.'

Nat got out, turned, and spoke to Guillaume through the open window. 'Nearly forgot,' he said, and tossed the Glock onto the passenger seat.

He climbed the steps. A steward closed the door behind him. The plane began to taxi before he could move. He looked to his right. Jack ran the length of the cabin to greet him, eyes swollen and red.

'Sorry, I'm late,' he said.

She smiled. Tears glistened on her alabaster cheeks.

'Where in God's name have you been?' she cried.

'Chaos,' he said. 'The wilder side of chaos.'

* * *

The church was silent. The acrid smell of gunpowder lingered in the air and the marble floor felt uncomfortably cold against his skin. Cashel had waited, patiently, until instinct told him it was safe to move. He spat a capsule of fake blood from his mouth and remained motionless a moment more. He sighed, sat up and pulled his blood-stained trousers to his ankles. The plastic bags taped to his thighs were spent. He discarded them, ripped the Kevlar from his body and thanked Christ he didn't take a hit above the neck. He fastened his belt and crept silently to the door. An unmarked car was waiting.

Chapter Eleven

*'And my heart falls back to Erin's Isle,
to the girl I left behind me.'*

Unknown

Jack was coming to terms with the situation. Coming to terms with the fact that she was embroiled in an Ian Fleming novel. She tried, desperately, to stay awake as the plane levelled off and made its final approach. Ignorant of their whereabouts, they gazed at the lush, green land below and wondered where in the world they were. Primitive looking huts lay strewn, randomly, across the grassy terrain. A decaying Hercules transporter plane, in camouflage livery, sat idle, overrun with small children. Oxen roamed free. They were escorted through the arrivals building: a makeshift affair, half brick, half corrugated iron. It was early. The sun was high. The mercury was nudging thirty. A heat haze clung to the horizon. A group of dark gentlemen in brightly coloured, striped shirts, sat sipping Coca-Cola by the bottle. A small man, sixty-something in years and immaculately dressed, trotted up to greet them.

'Welcome to Mombasa! Welcome, welcome!' he exclaimed. 'I do hope you enjoy your stay with us, you're very special people, I understand.'

Jack looked at Nat.

'Where the feck is Mombasa?' she whispered.

* * *

Cartwright was the British consul. He was old school with a colonial attitude and possibly the most polite man they had ever met. His leathery, wrinkled face oozed warmth and generosity. He made a gesture, as though dusting-off his pristine linen suit, and shook them vigorously by the hand.

'Come with me, come, come, we have a car waiting. It's alright, we'll look after you, you see if we don't! Few days here and I'll wager you'll be staying for life. We're a happy people here, you know, not much to speak of, material whatsits and so forth, but happy. Hope you brought some protection with you or you'll burn like toast, damned sun, gets intolerable sometimes, just wait for the rains, ha ha!, the rains, how splendid that can be, changes everything, you'll see! So, you two been married long, eh? I understand you're some young gun in the home office, Mr Pearson. Enjoy it, do you? All that malarkey? All those stick-in-the-muds in their suits? Can't say I...'

Cartwright concluded his soliloquy only when the car stopped outside the New Palm Tree Hotel on Nkrumah Road. He opened the door and escorted them inside. Mopping his brow with a neatly pressed handkerchief, his only plea was to be kept informed of their whereabouts. Within Mombasa, he told them, they were at liberty to do as they pleased, but any excursions farther afield needed permission. He was under orders, they were his responsibility, and he wanted to ensure their stay was a mutually enjoyable one.

He assured them that money was not an issue. Though none of them knew exactly how long they would be staying, everything would be billed to the consulate and a fund of cash would be made available for day-to-day living expenses.

'You'll enjoy spending here,' he said, 'we still have shillings, you know!'

As a final aside, he advised them to rest well before exploring their new surroundings, and politely took his leave. It was sound advice. The clock had yet to hit midday but the need for sleep was almost overwhelming. Nat and Jack repaired to their room and relished the cool, white tiles beneath their bare, aching feet. There was no air-conditioning, just an ineffective fan that hung from the ceiling and whirred as it circulated warm air around the room. A white mosquito net hung over the bed and a large bowl of fresh fruit took pride of place on the dresser.

Nat tipped the contents of his grip onto the bed, excited at the prospect of seeing what Guillaume may have packed for him. To his dismay, there were no surprises. Jack headed for the bathroom where the shower spluttered to life and doused her in tepid water, cool enough to quell the heat, yet warm enough to rinse the grime.

She emerged, dripping and naked, and lay on the bed, not even bothering to towel herself down, it was pointless. With one sweep of the arm, Nat stowed the contents of his grip, most efficiently, on the floor, and followed Jack's lead to the shower. He sat in the tub and allowed the water to pummel his head for a full twenty minutes before he emerged with a pudding-bowl hairstyle.

He sat on the bed and lit a Marlboro. It was probably the best tasting he'd ever had, as effective as a dose of Novocain. Jack took the cigarette from his hand and drew on it deeply, before handing it back with a look that would curdle milk. The arid, warm air caused the cigarette to burn her throat. She lay back and reached out to him, she wanted to sleep, she wanted to feel skin on skin, she needed to feel secure.

The last plume of smoke drifted lazily towards the ceiling, like the last, dying gasp of a genie's lamp. They lay in silence, their limbs entwined. In next to no time they were asleep, breathing as one.

* * *

The pain was not intense but aggravating nonetheless. A clean incision, with a sharp instrument, would not have woken him. He knew a clean cut would have brought him to his senses only when the last drops of life had oozed from his body. What he felt was dull. A dull object, tracing a line across his back intent on piercing his skin, like a butter knife trying to slice an unripened tomato. He opened his eyes. The sensation stopped. He turned swiftly and knocked Jack for a six.

'Jesus! I was only scratching your ba...'

He smiled and pulled her close. They watched from the balcony as the rising sun lit the underbelly of a storm rolling across the horizon. Lightning flashed within marshmallow clouds. Twenty minutes later, it was gone. The sun was up, as was the rest of Mombasa. They ordered breakfast: poached eggs, fresh fruit and a pot of Earl Grey before heading out.

Digo Road led them towards the port. Street vendors plied their trade with contagious grins, mouths full of brilliant white teeth, broken teeth and no teeth. Cashew nuts and cassette tapes. Braided necklaces and batik shawls.

The port itself was nothing more than a glorified slipway. A favoured spot for beggars and unfortunates who, like Jack and Nat, awaited the arrival of the ferry, keen to see what riches would spill from its decks. Slowly, it approached, lolling and chuffing, a tangled mass of wood and metal, strung together with wire and rope. Empty oil drums hung from the sides while the engine spluttered and coughed clouds of thick, black smoke across an azure sky. It docked with a thump, the bow doors crashed to the ground and hordes of people, buses and bicycles streamed onto terra-firma. A Nissan bus, horn blaring, screamed by with scant regard for anything in its path. Passengers clung to the roof; chickens clucked at the windows. It appeared to be driven by a goat. Jack gripped Nat by the arm, the excitement was at once overwhelming and confusing. They headed back up Digo, tailed by a three-legged dog with hungry eyes and a wagging tail.

It was time to leave. They had to be alone, away from the city, away from the noise, and away with themselves.

* * *

The following morning Nat met Cartwright at the consulate and procured the use of an ageing Land Cruiser. It was battered and bruised, the paintwork faded. He brushed the dust from the seats and turned the ignition. It started first time. 'Next best thing to a Land Rover!'

gushed Cartwright. Nat returned to the hotel, the Cruiser laden with spare fuel, drinking water, tinned groceries and a rifle. Bags packed, they set off, Jack behind the wheel.

Out of the city, the road to Samburu lost its tarmac dressing and cut a swathe through an obscenely green landscape, sparsely populated with acacias and the odd clump of shrubbery. Quietly at first, then without shame or inhibition, Nat sang, repeatedly, the only verse he knew of 'Born Free'. Jack slowed to a halt. They devoured the scenery in silence. A wilderness. Untouched. Unpopulated. Unscathed. The horizon stretched for miles. Save for the purr of the engine, it was blissfully quiet, almost silent. She smiled at Nat, rubbed his hand and set-off at a crawl. A lone zebra joined them, close enough to touch, head bobbing as it plodded alongside, smiling. Her eyes glazed over.

'He's beautiful,' she said.

'He's uhuru,' said Nat.

'What? And you're Captain Kirk?'

Nat smiled.

'Free.'

'Huh?'

'Uhuru. Means freedom.'

'Oh.'

'Let's go, Tsavo beckons.'

* * *

Two hours and eighty miles later they arrived at a village. It had no name and, so far as Nat could see, no reason to exist. There were no visible dwellings, just three stores, each built from breeze blocks with corrugated iron roofs. One sold groceries, another tyres and engine parts, the third, fresh fruit. A burned-out Bedford truck, minus wheels, stood forlornly out front. A gaggle of screaming, beaming kids rushed to greet Nat, arms outstretched, as he stepped from the Cruiser. He bought a case of Carlsberg, six bottles of Coca Cola and four bottles of rather suspicious-looking red wine that claimed to be the produce of Portugal. The kids faded in the rear-view mirror as they headed deep into the heart of Tsavo.

Nightfall was imminent. They had to make camp. Nat dragged the tent from the back of the Cruiser. It was tough, heavy canvas with wooden poles and worn ropes. It reminded him of his youth, camping in the Lakes as a cub-scout. They lit a fire, not too big, just enough to heat a billy and fend off the cold. The sky changed rapidly as the sun plummeted towards the horizon. Within minutes, the bright blue of day became the inky black of night. A night as black as pitch, a night dense enough to obscure a hand at arm's length.

Four tins of Fray Bentos bubbled and simmered over the fire. They huddled together, sipped Carlsberg and named stars. Crickets chirped. The stew was good. It wasn't homemade, it wasn't haute cuisine, but it was appropriate. Appetites sated, they doused the fire and retired to the minimal comfort of the tent.

* * *

Jack slept soundly, swathed in a false sense of security. Nothing would wake her, not even the rustling and grunting outside the tent. It was, however, enough to rouse Nat, who had been sleeping on tenterhooks for several weeks. He listened, tracking the sound as it passed by the tent. It stopped. He grabbed the Maglite and, cautiously, ventured outside. He stared, in a state of wonderment and awe, at the spectacle caught in the beam of the torch. One and half tons of amphibious meat stood before him. A baby hippo. Cute. A baby hippo without its mother. Dangerous. He retreated to the safety of the tent, lay down and curled an arm around Jack.

She woke first and shivered. She was cold, wet, soaked to the bone. She reached for Nat. He, too, was sodden, their sleeping bags, drenched. They wallowed in an inch and a half of water, unable to fathom the cause of the flood. Outside, the road on which they had travelled had completely disappeared. In its place lay a river of mud, a squelching mire which had already sucked the Cruiser down to its hub caps. They were lucky. It was not the advent of the rains, merely the result of an over-zealous storm. Nat waded through the bog, pulled a pair of steel treads from the roof of the Cruiser and wedged them under the rear wheels. They waited. By ten o'clock the sun had rendered the ground hard as rock and the 4x4 rolled effortlessly out of its rut. He spread a map across the bonnet and pointed out their location to Jack.

'We are somewhere here,' he said. 'I think we should go somewhere there.'

'There, is pretty feckin' big. Anywhere in particular?'

'Nope. That'll do,' he said, pointing to Amboseli.

* * *

They drove slowly. The heat was intense. He looked at Jack. For an Irish lass, she was doing well not to burn. Already, her skin was a golden brown, dried salt dusted her forehead. He passed the water and made her drink.

That night they made camp early. Amboseli was a day away. From there, suggested Nat, they could cross into Tanzania, and visit the Ngorongoro crater.

'What? But Nat, we don't have passports.'

'I know.'

'We won't have Cartwright to protect us.'

'I know.'

'What if something happens?'

'Don't know. We'll be fine. Trust me. We'll be fine.'

She did trust him, implicitly. She lit a fire while he rummaged through the provisions. Twilight wrapped them, briefly, in a velvety sky bejewelled with stars before they were plunged, once more, into darkness. Nat gazed at Jack, her sun-bleached hair scraped back in a ponytail.

'Jack,' he said, 'something I...'

'What's that?'

'Nothing, let's eat.'

He took the pot from the fire. Chilli bubbled like a witch's cauldron. It smelled hot. He dished it out and passed a plateful to Jack. Without thinking, he shovelled a spoonful of the devil's dinner into his mouth. The fire crackled and hissed as he spat it out, his taste buds charred to a cinder. 'Eejit!' she laughed. He put down his plate, cradled a bottle of beer, and squinted at Jack.

'What?' she said.

'Been thinking.'

'And?'

'Well, Lennie. He's dead. The business, it doesn't need me anymore. Actually, I don't need it.'

'So?'

'So, when we get back, I want you to do me a favour.'

'What's that then?'

'Be my wife. I want you... to be my wife.'

She stood, wrapped her arms around his neck and pulled him close. They swayed, gently, from side to side and said nothing.

* * *

Morning. Jack woke first. Laying on her back, she opened her eyes and smiled. It was, mercifully, dry. Dry but chilly. She stroked Nat's encircling arm. It was cold as ice. Rigid. She was lying in the arms of a dead man.

Exhausted, emotions spent, she fearlessly dragged herself outside, desperate for help, in need of support. Three men greeted her with welcoming eyes. They were Masai. Their presence did not strike her addled mind as odd, despite the fact they had no herd. Nor did she question where they had come from or how they had found her in a thousand miles of shrub. She raised an arm across her tortured brow, desperate to free herself from a state of desolation.

* * *

Patrick Ndambiki did his best to console her.

'Miss Jack, I cannot tell you why he died, but the coroner can, he will have the answers. Come now, we must move quickly. We must get him to Mombasa.'

'But… but why the hurry? I mean, can't we at least…'

'In this heat, I am sorry to say, he will not last. We must go, now.'

Patrick and his brothers wrapped the body in a sleeping bag and laid him gently in the rear of the Cruiser. Patrick took the keys from Jack.

'I will drive, Miss Jack. I am familiar with the route,' he said.

She did not question the fact that he was used to driving more than just cattle. Clouds of dust billowed in their wake, he wrestled with the wheel as the Cruiser bounced across the undulating terrain. She held on, her mind elsewhere, her spirit shattered. It was late afternoon when they arrived at the Consulate. Cartwright was waiting with the reassuring words of a beloved grandparent.

'It's Nat,' said Jack, tears welling up, 'he's... he's...'

Cartwright pulled her to his chest and patted her on the back.

'There, there, my dear.' He dabbed her cheeks with a pristine handkerchief. 'Fate is a fickle beast, but now you must be strong, be brave, think of the good times, the happy times. Think of how he made you smile, laugh, how he made you angry as hell. Am I making sense, or am I rambling like an old fool again?'

'You're so sweet, you...'

'Now shush. Come on, I think we could use a drink, don't you? A drop of something... medicinal, eh?'

She sipped a glass of Johnnie Walker while Cartwright cajoled her into regaling tales of their trip to Amboseli. Three floors below, in the bowels of the building. Nat's body lay on a trestle table.

* * *

An hour passed. Jack was on her third scotch when the coroner joined them. Muleba was a mild-mannered, softly-spoken man in his late fifties. He and Cartwright exchanged a knowing glance. He sat down, took Jack's hand and quietly explained that he could only issue a death certificate – he was not empowered to perform a post-mortem. Nat would go under the knife once his body had been re-patriated. He would travel back in a sealed casket, the following day. Jack finished her drink, thanked the consul for his support and returned to the hotel, to a cavernous bed, and a night without sleep.

Dawn. She showered, dressed and slowly packed what was left of Nat's belongings in his ageing grip. She refused to cry. Refused to give in to the tears. With just a few hours to go before her flight home, she wandered back along Digo Road, smiling and humming 'Born Free'.

* * *

The tannoy crackled. A muffled voice announced the final call for the KLM flight to Paris. Cartwright smiled, handed Jack her passport and took her gently by the elbow. She froze, rooted the spot. A thirteen-hour flight sitting a few feet above a coffin was no longer an option. She broke down. Cartwright made no attempt to force her. She could, he reassured her, travel whenever she liked.

They stood, side by side, staring at the plane, waiting for its departure. A few straggling passengers crossed the tarmac and raced towards the steps. Amongst them, a middle-aged couple, tanned but stressed. Neither Cartwright nor Jack would have recognised them. Panting, Ramon Hernandez and his diminutive wife made their way to first class. The door closed. Seconds later, the plane thundered along the runway and hurled itself into a cloudless sky. Jack wiped a tear from her cheek and gripped Cartwright's arm. Hernandez watched as the ground fell away. He smiled. Then grinned. Then laughed out loud. Cashel, the interfering cop, was dead. Pearson was twenty feet below him, in a sealed casket. That left Kowolski.

Chapter Twelve

*'And I am needing you here,
in the absence of fear.'*

Jewel Kilcher

'For the love of God, Patrick, if you don't move out the fockin' way, I will fockin' kill you!' screamed Cashel.

'But Leonard, my friend, we must be quick!' pleaded Patrick. 'It is nearly twelve hours now! You want him to wake with a brain like casava?'

'Just move and let your man, here, do his job! Where's Jack?'

'She is upstairs, with the consul.'

Muleba, dignified in his wire-rimmed spectacles, nonchalantly waved them aside as he spoke. He had a quiet, rumbling voice that came from the bowels of the earth.

'Quiet, please gentlemen. Now, what was the dose?' he asked Patrick.

'Five cc's! That's all you gave me, it was impossible to give more, I did not have it!'

'Excellent. And you administered it as instructed, here, behind his ear?'

'Yes! Yes! Please, will you see to him now?'

'Be calm, my friend, there is no need to worry. He may appear dead to you, but trust me, his heart still beats. He is strong.'

Muleba foraged deep within a battered leather Gladstone bag.

'I will need your help. First of all, remove his shirt. Now you, wipe his chest with this,' he said, and passed Patrick a swab doused with surgical spirit. 'Good. Now, hold him firmly, by the arms, he will react violently when he comes around. We do not want him injuring himself now, do we?'

Patrick and Cashel looked on as Muleba held aloft a steel syringe. It was not abnormally large, save for the needle. Three inches long and as tough as Toledo steel. Cashel swallowed and Patrick crossed himself as Muleba gently pumped the adrenaline the length of its shaft to ensure the chamber was free of air.

'Do not be alarmed,' he said, 'you will feel this more than him.'

Using the middle finger of his right hand, he traced the gaps between the ribs to the left of the sternum and held the syringe at a forty-five degree angle. The tip drew blood as it pierced the skin. Cashel winced.

'Gentlemen,' said Muleba, 'are we ready?'

He took a deep breath and, with both hands, rammed it between the ribs and into the heart. Quick as a flash, he forced home the plunger, pulled out the syringe and stepped back. Within a second of the adrenaline entering the bloodstream, Nat's body jerked to life. He sat, bolt upright, eyes wide, coughing, gasping for air. He looked shit. Muleba checked his pulse.

'Do not speak,' he said, 'breathe. Breathe slowly. Deeply.'

Gradually, Nat's breathing, and his colour, returned to normal.

'Water,' said Muleba.

He passed Nat a tumbler.

'Sip this. Do not gulp. Sip, little, little.'

Nat drank, sighed heavily and turned around.

'What the fuck are you doing here?! Where am I? What's…'

'Take it easy, fella,' said Cashel, grinning, 'you're okay.'

'But you're dead! I saw it, they shot you in… I left you…'

'Shhh. As you can see, I'm doing fine. Miracle, so it was.'

'What? But…'

'Five minutes,' said Cashel, 'sit still, relax. Five minutes.'

Nat bowed his head, sighed again and sipped from the tumbler. Muleba checked his pulse once more, smiled gently and closed his bag.

'I must go,' he said, 'I have to see the consul. Good luck.'

Nat, bewildered, looked quizzically at Patrick, then Cashel.

'So?' he asked.

Cashel cleared his throat.

'Nat, me old mate, meet Patrick. He's the fella that killed you.'

'Killed me?! What the…? I went to sleep, I was in the tent and I… hold on, where's Jack? Where the fuck is Jack?'

'She's fine! Honestly, she's fine, she's safe, don't worry yourself. Listen…'

Cashel pulled up a chair.

'Okay. Concentrate. Now, Hernandez. Three people he wanted dead.'

'You, me and Kowolski,' said Nat.

'Correct. Now, if you recall, we had no idea where Hernandez was, so, we had to figure out a way of getting him, to come to us.'

'I'm lost,' said Nat.

'Neufchatel. We set it up…'

'What?! We nearly fucking died! What do you…?'

'Hold your tongue, listen! We set it up, and we couldn't let him go home empty-handed, so I took the hit. With me out the way, we figured he'd concentrate on coming after you, and we were right.'

'But why here? It's a fucking long way to…'

'I know but, strange at seems, it made it easier for Hernandez. See, here you could die of a hundred things, so you could, not just a bullet in the head.'

'So, you got to me before he did.'

'In one.'

'And did he follow?'

'Oh aye, we know exactly where he is.'

Nat rubbed his eyes.

'So why don't you…'

'We can't, not here. We have to wait till he's on French soil.'

'So, when?'

'Soon. Right now, he's on his way back to Paris. As soon as he steps off that flight, he's ours.'

'What about Kowolski? If you take Hernandez, who's gonna…'

'Relax. Our friend Angelini is on the case. Leave that to him.'

Nat smiled, scratched his head and stared at Cashel.

'Life's too fucking complicated,' he said. 'Where's Jack?'

'On her way, too. You'll see her soon, so you will. How're you feeling?'

'Okay. Yeah, okay.'

'Good. Put your shirt on, we've a plane to catch.'

* * *

The pilot was smart, immaculate, debonair. He wore a starched white, linen shirt with epaulettes, white trousers and polished brogues. His cap sat at a jaunty angle atop his head. He removed his Wayfarers as they approached.

'You have got to be joking me,' said Cashel. 'What the fock is that?'

The pilot smiled.

'That,' he said, 'is a Dakota. Built in 1939. Don't worry, she flies like a bird.'

'I'll have to take your word for it. Come on, let's go.'

Nat looked baffled.

'Hold on,' he said, 'I don't get it. Where we going?'

'Nairobi,' said Cashel. 'Then a direct flight to Paris. We'll get there before Hernandez.'

* * *

There was an air of serenity in the tower. The air traffic controllers spoke quietly, calmly. Nat watched the tiny dots move like flies across the screen and listened for the occasional bleep. Cashel stood, hands clasped behind his back, watching the stack. An ATC called to him.

'Monsieur. C'est ici. Piste d'atterrissage deux, a gauche.'

Cashel looked to his left just as Hernandez' flight touched down.

'Let me know the gate, soon as you can. Patch me through to the pilot, now.'

He left the room, quickly, babbling into his radio, Nat in tow.

* * *

Hernandez was used to the privileges of travelling first class. A half-decent meal, free champagne and, naturally, the opportunity to disembark ahead of the hoi-polloi. He unbuckled his belt, grabbed his attaché case and clicked his fingers. Suzie followed. An eloquent stewardess smiled politely, wished him a pleasant stay in Paris and opened the cabin door. He failed to notice it shut behind him.

His footsteps echoed along the short, narrow gangway that led him to the gate. He turned the corner and stopped dead. Nine semi-automatic rifles were pointing at his head. Suzie whimpered, then began to shake. She clawed at her husband's arm, trying to get a grip. He shook her off. There was no yelling or shouting. Hernandez dropped his case as Cashel appeared behind the ranks of the Gendarmerie. He looked confused at first, then smiled as he raised his hands and slowly applauded. Cashel said nothing as Hernandez and his wife were cuffed and led away.

* * *

The apartment had been empty too long. It was cold and smelled damp, musty. Nat sneezed, lit a Marlboro and opened the fridge. The milk was off. He sneezed again. He sat and stared into space with nothing but the light from the street for company. He tossed the cigarette into the sink, laid down on the sofa and closed his eyes. It was still dark when the phone rang. Startled, he scrambled to answer it.

'It's me, Lennie.'

'What's up?'

'She's coming in this afternoon, Jack. I'll pick you up.'

Nat rubbed his chin and smiled. He had to get ready.

* * *

Kowolski sat huddled and unshaven, collar turned up against the cold. The rain lashed his face relentlessly. He blew on his hands in an effort to keep them warm. He harboured a grudge. A deep grudge. His lip curled at the thought of those responsible for his failure. Hernandez was gone. That left Cashel. He had to be taken care of. Alabama style. He pulled a Schmeiser from his inside pocket, screwed home the silencer and slid the sight into place. From the roof of the Arrivals building, he was sure he'd get the perfect shot.

* * *

The plane bumped and bounced as it hit the runway but still Jack slept. The other passengers scrambled for the overhead lockers, desperate to get their belongings. They stood impatiently as the plane slowly taxied towards the gate and came to a halt. One by one, they sat down again. The senior stewardess sauntered down the aisle, stopped at row twenty-two, and gently woke Jack from her slumber.

'Miss Caragh, you're off first. Must have friends in high places,' she said.

'Eh? I don't understand,' said Jack, half asleep.

'It's okay,' smiled the stewardess, 'come with me.'

* * *

The noise of the siren drew Nat to the window. There, on the street below, sat Cashel's filthy white Beemer. He hastened downstairs and slid quietly into the passenger seat. He looked at Cashel.

'Alright?' he said.

'Grand. All set?'

Nat stared at the raindrops as they trickled down the windscreen.

'You know this is going to scare the crap out of her, don't you?'

Cashel smiled.

'It'll be worth it,' he said. 'I've made arrangements. She'll be off first. You'll not be troubled by the other passengers.'

'Thanks. So! This is it.'

'Aye, this is it. The end. All over. Before you know it, you'll be back at your desk, drawing pictures or colouring-in, or whatever it is you do.'

Nat smiled.

'I think I'm through with that.'

Cashel floored the pedal and headed for 'de Gaulle.

* * *

They stood on the apron, side by side, hands clasped behind their backs. Twenty yards ahead, stood the plane. Nat focused on the door. The anticipation was unbearable. Eventually, it swung open and a solitary figure ventured forth. She looked small, vulnerable, scared. She grasped the handrail as the door closed quietly behind her and, head hung low, walked slowly down the steps.

The back of Cashel's head filled the gun-sight. The cross-hairs quartered his skull perfectly. Kowolski found it hard not to laugh. He lowered the gun, took a breath and raised it again. With a flick of the thumb, he released the safety catch and carefully wrapped his index finger around the trigger.

* * *

Jack reached the foot of the steps, brushed the sodden hair from her eyes and glanced up. At first, she looked petrified, then almost choked as she began to laugh and cry at the same time. Nat was transfixed, glued to the spot. He did nothing but grin as she ran towards him, arms flailing like saplings in the wind.

Cashel stepped forward. The bullet intended for his head, ripped through his shoulder instead. He spun as he tumbled towards the ground. Jack froze, rooted to the spot as Nat sprinted towards her, screaming at her to get down. Instead, she smiled and held out her arms.

A second bullet left the Schmeiser. Jack's expression turned to one of shock. A small, crimson mark appeared on her forehead. She stared, quizzically, at Nat for a moment, then fell, softly, silently, to the ground. Her body lay in a crumpled heap like a discarded rag doll.

The sky turned black. Nat dropped to his knees, shrouded in an overwhelming sense of insignificance.

The End

If you enjoyed this book, please let others know by leaving a quick review on Amazon. Also, if you spot anything untoward in the paperback, get in touch. We strive for the best quality and appreciate reader feedback.

editor@thebookfolks.com

www.thebookfolks.com

ALSO BY PETE BRASSETT

The DI Munro & DS Charlie West, Scottish murder mystery series:

Other titles:

Printed in Poland
by Amazon Fulfillment
Poland Sp. z o.o., Wrocław

53856002R00078